CW00644462

Her eyes met h

Shock coursed thro
going to earth. F
brother were one and the same man: It was
possible!

Time seemed suspended as Claire waited for
Brett to say something . . . and, when he didn't,
she frowned uncomprehendingly. With a sick
wave of shock, she realised that there wasn't
even a flicker of recognition in the cold blue
gaze which surveyed her with undisguised
hostility.

Dear Reader

The summer holidays are now behind us—but Mills & Boon still have lots of treats in store for you! Why not indulge yourself in long, romantic evenings by the fire? We're sure you'll find our heroes simply irresistible! And perhaps you'd like to experience the exotic beauty of the Bahamas—or the glamour of Milan? Whatever you fancy, just curl up with this month's selection of enchanting love stories—and let your favourite authors carry you away!

Happy reading!

The Editor

Liza Hadley gained a degree in English and European Literature and subsequently worked as both a social worker and a teacher before 'discovering' her real love—writing. Happily married with two sons, a large dog, two cats and a pet sheep, none of whom is particularly biddable, she thoroughly enjoys being able to create characters who, at least some of the time, behave as she wants them to. Living near the Lake District, she enjoys walking and reading.

Recent titles by the same author:

WILLING OR NOT

NOT SUCH
A STRANGER

BY
LIZA HADLEY

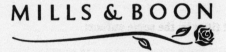

MILLS & BOON

MILLS & BOON LIMITED
ETON HOUSE, 18-24 PARADISE ROAD
RICHMOND, SURREY TW9 1SR

*First published in Great Britain 1993
by Mills & Boon Limited*

© Liza Hadley 1993

*Australian copyright 1993
Philippine copyright 1993
This edition 1993*

ISBN 0 263 78285 9

*Set in Times Roman 10 on 12 pt.
01-9311-49326 C*

Made and printed in Great Britain

CHAPTER ONE

'WHY the hell you had to take a couple of waifs and strays into the house right now, I don't know.'

The words, words which could only apply to her and Emily, were uttered with such raw aggression that Claire almost dropped the laden tea-tray she was holding, and the hand which had been poised to tap lightly on the oak-panelled door froze just before it reached its target.

She stood motionless in the hallway as a wave of hot humiliation swept over her. It was obvious that the speaker had no idea of her proximity, but that didn't prevent the appalling sense of mortification she felt on hearing herself and Emily described in such disparaging terms. *Waifs and strays* . . . like some forsaken orphans or pets!

My God! Was that how he thought of them?

Despising herself for doing it, she none the less peered cautiously through the narrow chink between door and frame. Duncan Cameron, her employer, had his back to her, but his brother, the man who had spoken, was hidden from sight.

'Claire is not a waif and Emily is not a stray, and I'd thank you not to refer to them as such,' Duncan remonstrated mildly.

'No? Yet obviously you don't know any more about her present circumstances than you would any abandoned bitch and her litter you'd picked up at the kennels.'

5

Claire flinched, reacting instinctively to the insulting terms, as if she were indeed the creature he described.

'I know as much as I need to know. Don't forget, Claire worked in my department for two years. I know that I like her and trust her and that's enough for me,' Duncan said firmly.

'Huh!' It was a derisive snort.

Claire appreciated Duncan's stout support, but it was small consolation for his brother's blatant contempt. She drew back from the doorway, no longer needing to see the stranger. Her imagination had already conjured a graphic image of him in her mind. His features didn't matter. She knew they were filled with raw anger and aggression.

He hated her. He'd never even met her, yet he hated her. Why?

Pain and anger made her throat contract in a sudden convulsion. What had she done to warrant such scorn from a man she'd never even met? And, given his total ignorance of her and her situation, what gave him the right to judge her so harshly? He had no right, no right whatsoever.

The tea-tray shook dangerously in her hands, threatening to set the crockery rattling and alert the room's occupants to her presence outside the door.

Gripping the edges tightly between her fingers, Claire retreated back along the passageway, every footstep an agony of tension as she tried to avoid the squeaking floorboards which would give her away.

'No eavesdropper ever hears good about themselves.' Her mother's prim advice filtered back to her. Maybe not, but surely few would ever hear themselves spoken of with such crude disdain by a stranger?

Back in the kitchen, palms slick with perspiration released the tray to let it slide noisily on to the scrubbed pine table and Claire allowed herself to sink weakly into one of the rush-seat chairs.

Why? Thoughts careered around her mind and then crashed into each other in utter confusion.

She knew from what Duncan had told her that his brother wanted peace and quiet...seclusion. That was why he was coming to Sandwood. The farmhouse's setting in the Lakeland hills, some half a mile from the nearest road, ensured that company was sought by choice, not endured by necessity.

Perhaps its solitary location was not enough. Perhaps he would have preferred the house to be empty rather than occupied by a resident housekeeper cum caretaker.

But the house was large. He must know that they need have little contact beyond the most basic day-to-day civilities. Why should her and Emily's presence here be such a source of abhorrence to him? Because that was what he'd made it sound like, total and utter abhorrence.

Colour drained from Claire's cheeks as she recalled his contemptuous words; 'waifs and strays'...'bitch and her litter'.

It revived the coarse insults her parents too had hurled at her. Their furious gibe, 'You're nothing but a cheap slut,' still echoed vividly in her ears.

When she'd returned from Australia, she'd spent a week listening to their outpourings of disgusted outrage. A week during which she'd tried to reason with them and at the same time come to terms with her own sense

of shock at her predicament and aching awareness that
she had been abandoned to face it alone.

After a week she had finally realised that no amount
of reasoning, or begging, was going to alter her parents'
views. Their initial anger and distress she could have
understood and coped with, but not the prospect of long-
term rejection and condemnation. When they had issued
their final ultimatum, she had left, unable to endure their
hostility and abuse any longer.

But she couldn't run away again. This time there was
no escape route open to her.

The nails of her fingers dug into her palms as a stab
of fear and then anger clawed at her insides.

Besides, why should she run away? She'd done no
harm to Duncan's brother. What right did he, a complete stranger, have to vilify her and make her feel so
utterly worthless?

He'd spoken as if she and Emily were an unwanted
package, not people at all. He was the brute, the one
who should be likened to an animal.

Immediately she recoiled from the simile. It was unfair
to animals. They attacked for a reason whereas he had
none. He didn't know them or anything about them.

Did he think that he was the only one to be put out
by this arrangement? How did he think *she* felt about
his arrival?

For the last few months, this house had been her and
Emily's home—more than a home, a haven. If Duncan
hadn't offered her the job of caretaker cum housekeeper
when he had, then she hardly dared think what would
have become of them. She loved it here, the rambling
incongruities of the house itself, the glorious beauty of

the surroundings, even the isolation. She didn't want, or need, company.

Did he—this appallingly rude, arrogant man—think that *she* welcomed his arrival any more than he did her incumbency?

But she at least had been prepared to accept his presence with tolerance and civility, whereas he obviously wasn't prepared to extend her either. He didn't deserve one scrap of consideration. Not one.

Claire jerked her head up as the door swung open and Duncan entered the room. Tension stiffened her body in its angular pose at the table as she held her breath, waiting to see the man who had spoken. But Duncan was alone.

'Ah! Tea.' He smiled, taking in the undisturbed tray still resting in front of her.

Claire blinked in brief confusion and then jumped up as she realised what he was referring to. 'It...it's cold,' she murmured. 'I was about to bring it up when the...the phone went. I'm afraid I forgot about it. I'll make a fresh pot.'

Her voice sounded jerky and, to her ears at least, the words had the ring of falsehood, albeit a small one, about them.

'Mmm, that smells good. What is it?' Duncan sniffed appreciatively at the delicious smell which filled the kitchen.

'It's just a casserole,' Claire said with a hint of dismissal, moving to fill the kettle at the sink. She'd prepared it especially with Duncan and his brother in mind, guessing that after the long journey from London they'd be ready for a meal.

Now she found herself fervently hoping they'd already eaten *en route*. Those contemptuous words she'd heard had ruined any appetite she might have had and the thought of sitting down and sharing a meal with the man who'd uttered them made her stomach clench in disgust.

But Duncan's next words banished even that forlorn hope.

'I'm sure my brother will love it.'

To Claire's ears, and perhaps his own, he spoke with false heartiness, as if to convince himself that a well cooked dish was all it would take to remove any constraint between them.

Claire's heart sank. Who was he kidding? He'd heard his brother's scorn, just as she had, and probably more besides. An earth remover wasn't going to shift that lout's opinion, let alone a few spoonfuls of stew!

'But you'll stay and have some too?' she asked with more than a touch of desperation, violet eyes widening in mute appeal. She knew Duncan had to drive back tonight. But not yet. Please not yet!

Duncan gave a slight, apologetic shrug. 'I only wish I could, but I must be back in London before midnight. I've a plane to catch at six o'clock tomorrow morning.'

Of course! The demands of big business! And they didn't come much bigger than Atlas Engineering, the company owned by Duncan's family, which was involved in construction projects all over the world.

Claire's dismay must have been evident in the downcast curve of her mouth and the stricken look in her eyes, for Duncan continued with deliberate cheerfulness. 'Don't worry, Brett'll eat my share easily.'

'Brett?'

Her single word had a sharp, discordant sound, drawing a look of enquiry from Duncan.

'Yes, Brett. Why?'

Claire struggled to get the jangling reaction of her nerves under control. Good lord! There were thousands of men called Brett in this country alone. If she was going to go into convulsions every time the name was mentioned, she would be perpetually in a state of shock.

'N...nothing,' she stammered, swinging away from him to busy herself with warming the teapot. Anything to keep her trembling fingers occupied. 'You...you hadn't mentioned his name before, that's all.'

Lies...more lies, the voice of her conscience mocked her, but she thrust it aside. It really didn't matter what Duncan's brother was called. Tom, Dick, Harry? Any would do equally well for, whoever he was, he wasn't *the* Brett, the man whose vivid image she had carried in her mind's eye for the last fifteen months, that image almost her only memory of him. Almost, but not quite.

'Hadn't I?' Duncan's voice sounded behind her. 'An oversight on my part; I'm sorry. Anyway, he's here now. Meet him for yourself.'

Claire felt the draught from the door opening whip round her slender ankles and ruffle the hem of her calf-length skirt. All her senses seemed suddenly to have gone on danger alert and she felt the hairs on the back of her neck prickle.

A shiver of antagonism fluttered down her spine, making it stiffen with a hint of defiance as she turned to face the man who had labelled her and Emily ignominious 'waifs'.

She gazed across the room and every drop of colour drained from her skin as her eyes met his. Shock coursed through her body, like electricity going to earth. To save her life, she couldn't have moved...couldn't even have blinked to break the invisible thread which trained her eyes to his. Brett Jarrett and Duncan's brother were one and the same man! It wasn't possible!

The teapot slipped in her fingers, sending a scalding torrent of tea to the floor and splashing on her skirt and legs.

'Claire... Claire... whatever's the matter? Have you hurt yourself?' Duncan hurried across the room to take the teapot from her numb fingers.

Like an unresisting child, she allowed him to manoeuvre her into a chair, barely even aware of his ministrations.

Time seemed suspended as she waited for Brett to say something... and, when he didn't, she frowned uncomprehendingly. With a sick wave of shock, she realised there wasn't even a flicker of recognition in the cold blue gaze which surveyed her with undisguised hostility.

'Is that helping?'

Claire tugged her eyes away from Brett's long enough to stare down at Duncan kneeling on the floor and applying a dripping wet cold sponge to her leg.

Her body felt numb, completely numb, from the top of her head to the tips of her toes. Neither the scalding tea nor the icy water seemed to be making any impression on flesh petrified by shock. She felt nothing except an overwhelming sense of horror.

He didn't even recognise her!

Had she made some hideous mistake? Her eyes flicked briefly back to the figure still framed in the doorway. No, no, there was no mistake. It was Brett...Brett Jarrett.

How could she not have known him when his image was as deeply etched in her mind as her own?

Tall, lean, superbly male, he didn't even need to move to make his presence felt. Brett Jarrett emanated uniqueness the way other people exhaled carbon dioxide. It was as natural to him as breathing.

No matter that his clothes weren't the designer attire he'd been wearing when she'd met him—now faded denims hugged the muscled length of his legs and an Aran sweater snugly contoured the broad arc of his shoulders; she couldn't have failed to recognise him.

Equally obvious was the fact that the remembrance wasn't mutual.

Claire had no idea how long she stared at him, how long it took for that appalling realisation to fully penetrate her thoughts. The moment seemed to stretch on and on, rooting her feet to the floor and cleaving her tongue to the roof of her mouth in agonised silence.

Somehow, by an almost superhuman effort of will, she tore her eyes from Brett's to mumble in Duncan's direction, 'It...it's fine...fine... Please don't worry.'

'Of course I'm worried,' he said tautly. 'That scald must have been worse than I thought. You nearly went into shock just then.'

She'd gone into shock all right, though not because of any scald. But perhaps it was better that Duncan should attribute her reaction to that rather than to seeing his brother.

'Maybe I should take you to hospital to get it checked.'

'No...no.' Immediately she brushed the suggestion aside. 'Honestly, it feels OK now. I...I'll just go and change.'

With a firmness of purpose she was far from feeling, she stood upright. 'See...no damage.' She flexed her leg and began to move towards the door.

The exit which she was so desperate to make necessitated brushing past Brett. Please let him move out of the way, she begged silently. But her mute plea went unanswered as he remained resolutely in the doorway, one arm carelessly bridged against the jamb, blocking her way.

Involuntarily, she trembled, suddenly assaulted by the potent male scent she remembered so vividly. Without warning, her senses clamoured for an infusion of the heady pleasures he had introduced them to. Her pupils widened on the taut thigh muscles outlined by flesh-hugging jeans.

'So you're Claire,' he drawled.

His voice vibrated against her ear-drum, but not with the silky sensuality it had once done. It was a stranger's voice. A stranger addressing a stranger. Oh, God! Did he really not know her...not at all?

'So you're Claire'. How had he managed to make three such innocent words so heavy with implication? As a greeting it ranked more as an insult.

A spurt of pride came to her aid and she lifted violet eyes to his blue ones. Whatever else she might or might not deserve from Brett Jarrett, insults weren't among them.

'Yes, I'm Claire,' she agreed with a dignity that was all the more noticeable for its contrast with his drawled taunt.

Then, because every second she held his sardonic gaze unleashed a torrent of memories into her bloodstream, memories too graphic to be kept hidden for long, 'Would you mind moving aside? I'd like to go and get changed.'

'Of course,' he agreed, letting his arm fall with such nonchalant grace that it refuted any suggestion that he'd been barring her way in the first place.

Claire took the stairs two at a time, desperate now to reach the haven of her bedroom. Her legs felt like jelly and her breath was being torn from her lungs in great, ragged gasps.

There'd been shocks aplenty during the last fifteen months, but somehow this was the worst of all...the very worst. If she'd known...suspected for one moment that Brett Jarrett was Duncan Cameron's brother, she'd have... What would she have done?

It would be sheer stupidity to say she'd have run away when she'd spent over a year desperately trying to contact him, or, perhaps more accurately, trying to get him to contact her.

Only she knew the black, sleepless hours she'd spent, lying awake in her bed, wondering why he didn't respond to any of her letters.

And all the time, he'd been Duncan's brother! Why hadn't he told her of the family link from the beginning? Why had he kept it secret?

Claire reached the sanctuary of her room and forced herself to shut the door quietly behind her. She leaned back against it, closing her eyes and hugging her arms to her in an agony of pain and confusion.

Never in all her wildest dreams or nightmares of imagining what meeting him again would be like had she considered for one moment that he wouldn't even recognise her. Nothing had prepared her for that appalling possibility.

Her eyes flickered open and she saw her image reflected in the full-length mirror of the wardrobe on the opposite side of the room.

Had she changed so much? True, her hair had grown out of its neat bob to tumble in silvery blonde curls around her shoulders, and she'd gained some weight, losing the gamine look to more feminine curves at breast and hip. The tan had gone too, her skin returned to its more customary English pallor, but they were hardly changes that rendered her unrecognisable. Not to anyone who knew her well.

I suppose it all depends on what you mean by 'well', Claire considered with a pang of bitterness. Because of course Brett didn't really know her *well* at all. You couldn't call a week's acquaintance knowing someone well.

A week's acquaintance! How formal that sounded and how inadequate to describe the idyllic time they'd spent together. It suggested nothing more than a casual, holiday romance, but there'd been nothing casual about her feelings for Brett. She'd loved him almost from the moment she'd set eyes on him, loved him with a fierceness and a passion which had shocked her with its raw intensity.

And even when she'd come to realise, from his refusal to answer any of her letters, that the time they'd spent together couldn't possibly have meant as much to him as it had to her, she had never thought he could have forgotten her completely!

A slight movement in the corner of the room drew Claire's eyes to the cot and its occupant. Treading carefully so as not to wake her sleeping daughter, she moved to stand beside it, her anguished expression softening a little as she looked down at her.

Perhaps she was overlooking one crucial factor where memory was concerned. For almost every day of the last fifteen months, she had carried with her a flesh-and-blood reminder of the week she and Brett Jarrett had spent together. What better reminder of that brief, wonderful week than their daughter?

Claire closed her eyes as memories flooded in torrents through her mind, bouncing off each other in painful, turgid reverberation, and transporting her back in time to that fatal first meeting.

It all started with Great-Aunt Helen's twenty-first birthday present to her. Great-Aunt Helen—the black sheep of the family; at least, that was how Claire's mother always described her.

Helen had married young and made what was coyly referred to in those days as 'a good match', meaning she had married into money.

In the eyes of Claire's parents, that was the only sensible thing she had ever done but Helen always assured Claire that, 'The money didn't matter a hoot'. She had loved her husband and would have married him if he had been penniless.

When he had died after only a few years together, Helen had vowed never to marry again. She had been fortunate at least to have been left with sufficient income to make a regular job unnecessary and, since she had no children to keep her at home either, travelling became her passion.

When Claire had been growing up, Helen had seemed a wildly romantic figure, poignantly touched by just the right degree of tragedy. She had appeared intermittently in Claire's life, always, it seemed, *en route* from or for some far-flung place on the atlas, and, much to the disapproval of Claire's practically minded parents, she had encouraged her great-niece's love of art and poetry and literature, assuring her that feeding the soul was just as important as feeding the body.

As a child, Claire had listened spellbound to the details of her travels and later they had exchanged long, affectionate letters. Her great-aunt's had been full of humour and vivid descriptions and Claire had done her best to make her job as a secretary with Atlas Engineering in London sound as interesting as possible.

On Claire's twenty-first birthday, Helen had given her a sum of money, with the very specific instructions that she was neither to save it nor buy anything practical with it but was to use it to do something that was both fun and frivolous.

It wasn't a huge sum of money but it was certainly more than Claire had ever possessed before and she'd decided to use it, much to Helen's approval and her parents' disapproval, to do some travelling of her own.

Claire had been fascinated by Australia ever since she was a child and was determined to visit it one day. Helen's windfall had provided her with the perfect opportunity.

Duncan Cameron, then her boss at Atlas Engineering, had been more than generous. He'd refused to accept her resignation and promptly offered her three months' unpaid leave instead, and even a week's use of one of the company's apartments in Sydney, where Atlas Australia was based.

It was the first time Claire had ever been abroad; the demands of the general store which her parents owned and ran in a small Yorkshire village meant that holidays had always been limited to an occasional weekend at the coast.

From the minute she'd arrived at Heathrow airport she knew exactly why Helen loved travel so much. Excitement had uncurled within her at the sight of all those aeroplanes bound for far-away places. For the first time in her life she'd felt completely free, able to do anything, go anywhere, and the limitless possibilities were intoxicating.

A kind of wild impetuosity had gripped her at that moment, unshackling the staid reserves of her cautious Yorkshire upbringing. She felt independent and adventurous, adult and sophisticated in her smart new clothes and sporting the sleek new haircut she'd treated herself to.

Australia was everything she'd dreamed it would be; she loved the savage grandeur of Ayers Rock, the tropical paradises off the north-east coast, the wilderness of the national parks. Wherever she went, she was touched by the raw beauty of the landscapes and by the fierce, sometimes abrasive energy of the people. Two months into the trip, confidence growing along with a healthy, glowing tan, Claire had arrived in Sydney.

She'd collected the keys for the apartment from the company office in the late afternoon and spent the next few hours luxuriating in the facilities which it offered. The need to make her money stretch as far as possible meant that she'd often stayed in the cheapest accommodation available, the type of accommodation where spacious showers and big, circular Jacuzzis were definitely not the order of the day.

Revelling in the sensation of red-hot jets of water pummelling her body and rinsing the dust of several days' travelling from her hair, Claire had blessed Duncan for his thoughtfulness in allowing her the use of the apartment for the week she was to spend in the city.

Afterwards she'd changed into a brightly printed strapless dress and went to stand on the balcony, leaning out over its white rail and watching a brilliant ochre sun set over Sydney's jagged skyline.

It had been late November and the cool breeze of evening brought a welcome relief from the oppressive heat of the day. It ruffled the silky strands of Claire's silvery blonde hair and lifted them off her neck in gently refreshing waves.

In the courtyard down below, a party was in progress; music played, couples danced, groups of people laughed and chatted. A palm-topped bar had been set up to dispense drinks. Claire had eyed it longingly, wondering if she dared go down and request a long, cool glass of fruit juice.

There were no supplies in the apartment and, while she wasn't worried about the lack of food, the prospect of a drink other than iced water was enticing.

A couple of months before she would probably have ignored her thirst, not daring to impose on a private party. But she'd learned in the last few weeks that Australians had little time for inhibitions and reserve. If you wanted something, you asked for it. Not to do so wasn't considered manners but a peculiar kind of pride in self-deprivation.

Thus a few minutes later she'd found herself perched on one of the high stools beside the bar, sipping at a tall glass of pineapple juice and lemonade readily dispensed by one of the young waiters.

He'd laughed when she'd explained that she wasn't one of the guests and offered to pay for the drink.

'Hey! If we asked everyone here for their invite, there'd be an awful lot of red faces,' he said, obviously amused by her concern. 'Have as many as you like. No one'll notice.'

Claire had no intention of having more than one, but his invitation made her feel more relaxed, not so out of place. She sipped slowly then, glancing round at the assorted guests with casual interest.

She saw him first, of course. Brett Jarrett was that sort of man, the sort who effortlessly attracted attention, especially of women.

Individual features evaded description for it wasn't the detailed minutiae which drew the attention immediately but the overall impression of supreme assurance and absolute power. The sort of assurance and power which belonged only to those who seemed never to have known a single moment's doubt about their own supremacy in any sphere.

His casual suit in muted olive-green, teamed with a black silk shirt, suited him perfectly. It drew the eye to every inch of the superb physique it covered, eloquently telling of the lean, muscled hardness which rippled beneath.

He exuded sex appeal. Not the too perfect appeal of a male model, but a much more dangerous kind, the wild, uninhibited kind which every woman longed to tame, even while knowing that domestication was impossible.

Lightly rumpled jet-black hair invited a smoothing hand, the taut angle of his cheekbone beckoned a caress, and the mouth, hard and uncompromising above a shadowed jawline, lured with heady promise.

He was lounging back against the ornate white rail which surrounded the swimming-pool, the powerful lines of his body set in an innately graceful arc. A number of blatantly adoring females were gathered around him, yet for all that he stood alone, indifferent to their homage. He looked bored, like a man with a jaded appetite who found nothing to tempt him in the feast spread out before him.

When vivid blue eyes clashed fleetingly with hers, Claire felt a sensation strike her akin to what she imagined a bolt of lightning must feel like. It entered the very top of her head and speared her to the ground. She had never been so shocked in all her life.

And when he smiled lazily at her, it contained such lethal promise that Claire almost felt her toes curling. Instinctively she wanted to look away, to show by her cool disdain that she was not a woman who invited, or responded to, the suggestive smile of a stranger.

But somehow she found herself smiling back at him, and the next moment he was crossing the paving towards her, moving with the prowling fluency of a sleek black panther, ignoring the trailing female fingers which would have held him back. He was coming not just *to* her, but *for* her, Claire realised on a sudden wave of panic.

When he was beside her, so near that she could smell the heady male fragrance of him, his hand reached out to take the glass from her fingers and set it down, then closed round her waist and drew her into the small cluster of dancing couples.

His body was lean and hard as he pulled her against him, moving with an easy rhythmic grace.

Tremors of uncertainty rippled through her at their intimate proximity. She could feel the hard length of his thighs moving against her own, the firm stomach muscles beneath her fingers, the muscled strength of his chest as it brushed against her breasts.

'Isn't it usual to ask a lady first if she wants to dance?' she enquired lightly, laughing, professing nonchalance.

'I did ask,' he returned smoothly, his voice as darkly seductive as the rest of him. 'And you said yes.'

'I did?'

He nodded and in the shadowy darkness his eyes glittered down at her. 'You know you did. More explicitly than any words could have done.'

The supreme arrogance of the statement didn't matter because she knew it was true. In some strangely telepathic way, when their eyes had locked, she had said yes.

A whole series of responses made trip-wires of her senses, jolting them into startled reaction. What else had her body told him? she wondered dazedly as velvet fingers moved over the bare flesh of her shoulders, sending hot, thermal streams shooting through her veins.

Instinctively she knew that Brett Jarrett was dangerous. Even dancing with him was like playing with fire. Normally an innate wariness would have sent her running a mile but that night she hadn't run, hadn't even turned and walked away.

That choice was her downfall. It brought the dull but safe world she had inhabited until then crashing down about her ears, all in the blink of an eyelid. When she looked again, everything had changed. Brett Jarrett had just become the axis on which her world pivoted.

CHAPTER TWO

'BRETT'S—er—gone to unpack,' Duncan explained when Claire re-entered the kitchen some time later.

Gone to avoid her, more like. Claire acknowledged the painful truth. To Brett Jarrett she was no more than a stranger and a wholly unwelcome one at that.

'How's your leg?'

'Oh...fine,' Claire lied. Like the rest of her, it felt battered and bruised, as though she'd just received a severe beating. But it was her emotions which had taken the brunt of the assault, not her body.

Duncan shifted uncomfortably in his seat and his fingers began a monotonous drumbeat on the table. Normally relaxed and calm in his manner, he looked unusually ill at ease. 'Claire,' he began, weighting the word self-consciously, 'I haven't been entirely fair to you.'

'Haven't you?' she managed, his words barely penetrating the misty aura of confusion and pain which had enveloped her. She tried to make sense of what he was saying and failed. As far as she was concerned Duncan was one of the fairest men she'd ever met. He'd offered her a job and a home when she'd needed both desperately and she would be eternally grateful to him for it.

'No, I haven't. I never really explained why Brett wanted to come to Sandwood right now.'

Perhaps he hadn't, but neither had she asked. Preoccupied with her own problems, she'd spared little thought for those of a stranger. When Duncan had said his brother needed some peace and quiet and wanted to spend a few weeks at the farmhouse, she'd assumed he simply needed a little rural tranquillity, a rest from the pressures of business and city life.

'Brett was involved in an accident.'

Instinctively a jolt of pain shot through her, incisive and penetrating as a stab wound. Brett . . . hurt? 'An accident? When?'

Duncan's brow furrowed in painful recollection. 'Over a year ago now . . . in Australia. Brett heads the company's operations over there.'

Numbly Claire absorbed yet another shock. Brett was head of Atlas Australia, yet he'd never mentioned that either. Why?

The question was lost as she listened, appalled, to Duncan's continuing account of the accident.

'A light aircraft that Brett was flying came down in a storm. He was badly injured . . . nearly died, in fact. He's recovered now, of course, physically at least, but he was in a coma for several months with severe head injuries and it's left him with some memory loss.'

Amid the horror of learning how close Brett had come to dying, a shard of hope impinged itself on Claire's mind and a pulse began to throb restlessly in her throat. 'Memory loss? You mean amnesia?'

Duncan nodded. 'That's right. I'm afraid Brett gets rather impatient about it though the doctors have assured him that, given time . . . and peace and quiet, his memory should return naturally. Hence his stay here.'

Crescent-shaped nails dug deeply into the palms of her hands as she tried to assimilate what Duncan was telling her. The possibility that Brett might be suffering from amnesia had never occurred to her. Why should it? But now it began to make a strange kind of sense.

She swallowed convulsively, her expression strained and tense. 'Do you mean——?'

Duncan saw her stricken look and misinterpreted it. 'It's nothing for you to worry about,' he hastened to reassure her. 'Brett hasn't forgotten anything important. He recognises all the family...people who matter to him. It's just a few minor bits and pieces he can't recall, mainly events in the weeks preceding the accident. Nothing that need concern you. I just thought I should warn you about it, that's all. Brett gets rather impatient at times though the doctors have assured him it should all come back if he just gives it time and stops trying to force it.'

'Brett hasn't forgotten anything important... people who matter to him.' A wave of dizziness swept over Claire as Duncan's words set up an agonised tattoo inside her head. Desperately she clung to her one tiny shred of hope. 'But he can't remember what happened before the accident...people...people whom he...he may have met?' She persisted with a kind of fierce urgency.

Duncan gave her an odd look. 'Really, my dear, you sound quite anxious. There's no need. As far as we know Brett hasn't forgotten anyone. I doubt he's even forgotten anything important. The problem isn't so much the memory loss itself as Brett's attitude to it. He hates having to accept other people's accounts of what happened during that time, however inconsequential the details may be.'

That, Claire could understand. Brett was a man who shaped his own destiny, made his own decisions. Having to accept second-hand accounts of events he had been involved in could never be anything but poor consolation to him.

Her punch-drunk brain feverishly tried to assemble a logical sequence of thoughts. Brett's amnesia *must* extend back to the time they had met. Surely it was the only possible explanation for his blatant failure to identify her? There hadn't even been a flicker of recognition in his eyes when he had looked at her.

And if that was true, what else might be true? If the accident had occurred *before* she left Australia, perhaps he'd never received her letters, perhaps...

Burgeoning hope fluttered like a frantic, netted butterfly inside her breast.

'When... when did you say this accident happened?'

'Just over a year ago... last February, in fact.'

Why did hopes collapsing leave so little debris in their wake? Nothing to show, no evidence to betray their destruction, and yet Claire felt as if a volcano had just imploded inside her. Last February... Some two months *after* she left Australia.

Had she really believed that the shattered fragments of her dreams could be reassembled just like that?

For the briefest of moments she had allowed her hopes to flourish with the extravagance of blooms in time-lapse photography and now she'd seen them dashed like fragile crystal.

Of course Brett had received her frantic letters. He hadn't been oblivious of them; he'd simply chosen to ignore them.

Why *had* he withheld the truth from her about his relationship with Duncan and his involvement with Atlas

Engineering? Her mind fought against acceptance of the answer, but there could only be one possible explanation. From the beginning Brett had contrived to ensure that she couldn't contact him after she left Sydney.

Claire was aghast now at her own foolishness. She had been caught up in a frenzy of love and passion, and all sense of reality had flown out of the window during the week they'd spent together. Knowing so little about the practical details of Brett's life—where he worked, what he did, not even his telephone number—hadn't mattered to her then.

The only thing she had known was where he lived. He hadn't bothered to keep that secret, she realised on a wave of anguish, because letters were so easy to toss in a waste-paper bin. No doubt that was where all hers had ended up!

His accident changed nothing. All it meant was that now her banishment from his life was complete. He didn't even remember her.

Duncan frowned at her stricken expression. 'I've obviously worried you and that wasn't my intention at all. What I'm trying to say, not very successfully, evidently, is that you may find Brett a little . . . difficult to get along with at first. He wasn't aware that Elspeth and I had appointed a housekeeper, you see, and he . . . well, to be frank . . . he was expecting to be alone here. So if he is a little . . . impatient at times, don't let it worry you. It really isn't anything personal.'

Duncan exhaled an audible sigh of relief, as if glad to have got an awkward explanation out of the way.

He wasn't to know that almost every word sliced a rent in Claire's heart. 'Difficult . . . impatient'; that was putting it mildly. Brett hated her being here!

Nothing personal! If she had been a stranger to him, such hostility would have been difficult to endure. Filled with memories of the intimacies they had shared, as she was, it would be intolerable.

Half an hour later, Duncan had gone. Claire listened to the sound of his car engine receding down the rough track which led to the main road and felt the tension inside her rise to almost hysterical proportions.

Her heart beat like a sledge-hammer against her breastbone at the prospect of facing Brett alone. What on earth was she going to tell him?

The truth? It seemed logical and yet how could she, just like that? He was so sure he'd never set eyes on her before. How could she baldly announce that they had once been lovers, that they had a six-month-old daughter asleep upstairs? He would think she was mad, or lying, or both.

If he demanded proof, she couldn't give him any. She didn't even have any photographs of the holiday. The bag containing her camera and films had been lost on the journey back from Australia and never recovered.

And what reason did she have for thinking he'd be interested in Emily's existence anyway? Some of her letters must have reached him before the accident. Although she'd never actually told him of her pregnancy in writing, if he'd read them at all he must have guessed the reason behind her desperate requests that he should contact her.

Faced with the answer to that painful question, she found the reckless temptation to grab Emily and escape like Duncan in the small car he'd provided her with almost irresistible. But where to?

She couldn't go to her parents and the little money she'd managed to save during the last few months wouldn't buy more than a few days in a hotel. In truth she had nowhere to go.

Panic clutched at her throat as the kitchen door swung open and Brett came into the room. She should have been better armed. Seeing him once should have modified the second wave of shock his appearance brought with it, but it didn't.

Cold fingers inched down her spine as the shadowy figure from her dreams stood before her, more powerful and vivid than any memory.

Strange paradoxes danced before her eyes, like flickering images on a screen. Brett shouldn't be here, in the large, homely kitchen of a Lakeland farmhouse. The pictures inside her head placed him in such totally different locations: in hip-hugging shorts and T-shirt beneath a sun-drenched sky, black hair whipped back by the breeze as he took the helm of a yacht in Sydney's magnificent harbour, or behind the wheel of an open-topped sports car, driving them to the spectacular Blue Mountains.

Nor should he be glaring at her with the hostile eyes of a stranger. Bright, dazzling memories assaulted her, of Brett laughing when she pulled a face during a wine-tasting session at Hunter Valley, of Brett whispering silkily in her ear as he drew her into his arms, of Brett's mouth, moist and hungry, covering hers in the dark intimacy of his bedroom.

She swallowed deep and hard, ruthlessly squashing the memories, and reaching out trembling fingers to fiddle nervously with a teaspoon lying idly on the table.

'Duncan's gone,' she announced unnecessarily in a desperate bid to break the silence.

'I know.'

Another elongated moment of tension followed before Brett said roughly, 'It bothers you, doesn't it? Being alone here with me.'

Claire's head jerked up. 'No! Why should it?' The denial was instinctive, a defensive reaction against the coldly inquisitive look he was slanting down at her.

Uncompromising blue eyes met hers. 'Why lie? You're bloody terrified. Look at you! You're trembling even now. Don't bother trying to deny it. You've been looking at me strangely from the moment Duncan introduced us.'

Claire thrust her betraying hands beneath the table out of sight. 'Have . . . have I?'

She hadn't considered beforehand what direction any conversation between them might take. She'd been too stunned by his arrival at Sandwood to think beyond that moment and now she had nothing in reserve.

He wanted an explanation for her shocked reaction and she had none to offer. Except perhaps the truth . . .

Hastily she brushed the possibility aside. No, she couldn't do that. Not until she'd had time to consider the implications.

'Yes, and I'd like to know why.'

'I . . . I really don't know what you're talking about.'

Jet-black brows winged together impatiently. 'I think you do and I'd rather we got it out in the open now. You're frightened of me for some reason and I want to know why.'

Disconcertingly he came to stand before her, nudging one denim-clad thigh on to the edge of the table and folding his arms. The faded blue of his jeans blurred into the solid length of thigh they encased. Whatever physical debilitation Brett might have experienced following the accident, he was over it now, Claire acknowledged irrelevantly.

'What has Duncan told you about me?' The demand was cold, clinical almost.

'Nothing,' she murmured, confused.

Brett's eyebrows rose sceptically. 'Nothing? I find that hard to believe. He must have said something.'

Claire frowned, trying to grasp where his questions were leading. 'Only that you were involved in an accident.' It must be safe to admit that at least.

'That's all?'

'And that you've suffered some…some memory loss.' Memories of me included. An almost irrepressible urge rose up inside her to spill out the truth, however shocking it might be. There was a strange unreality about this whole conversation. It was bizarre…crazy. She felt deceitful knowing something that Brett didn't.

'Ah!' The sound was a rough purr of satisfaction. 'So that's it. I suppose he told you all the details.'

'Not all of them, no.'

'But enough to frighten you to death?' Brett bit out angrily. 'Is that why you're so bloody terrified? Did you think you were going to be sharing the house with a madman?'

'No, of course not,' Claire denied hotly, suddenly realising what Brett was insinuating. He thought she regarded him as *dangerous*!

The idea was ridiculous, but it made her see that Duncan had been right. Brett was far more irascible about his memory loss than she'd realised.

Did that make her decision to withhold the truth, for the moment at least, better or worse? Would the shock of her announcement add to his trauma or provide the key to that locked door inside his mind? She had no way of knowing the answer.

'No?' One black brow arched sceptically. 'You'd be surprised how many people associate psychological trauma with mental illness.'

'Well, I'm not one of them,' Claire retorted. 'Whatever misconceptions you've encountered from other people, they're not shared by me.'

Her terse assertion momentarily silenced him and he stared at her, the hard angles of his face set in a thoughtful expression.

'Then if it's not that, it must be something else that's nettling you. What, I wonder?'

Blue eyes raked over her in insolent appraisal, making Claire pale.

He knows... he's guessed, she thought in panic.

'If it's not anything Duncan told you, then there must be another reason for your reaction,' he mused, half to himself.

His low, sardonic growl startled her. 'You overheard what I said to Duncan in the library... some of it at least... didn't you?'

It wasn't what she had been expecting. 'How did you know?' she asked, too stunned to deny it.

There was a slight shrug of broad shoulders beneath the creamy Aran sweater. 'I thought I saw a movement in the mirror. I didn't give it much thought at the time, but it was you, wasn't it?'

Of course! The mirror opposite the door. Nausea welled up in Claire's stomach as she realised with sick certainty that he *had* seen her. God! How must she have looked, crouching there? 'I...I didn't mean to overhear.'

Black brows winged upwards in blatant mockery. 'You mean it happened by accident?'

'No! I was bringing you some tea and I heard what you said about me...what you called me...' Her voice trailed off and she shuddered as she recalled the debasing terms he'd used. *'Waif...stray...bitch.'* It had been bad enough when she had thought it was a stranger uttering those terms; knowing it was Brett made the memory all the more piercing.

A flash of violet iris challenged his blue. Why should her conscience be stricken? She'd done nothing wrong. 'I didn't stay long, I can assure you. I was appalled...disgusted by what I overheard.'

Brett's hard-edged mouth was uncompromising. 'You can hardly expect me to apologise for saying something in confidence that was never intended for your ears. You eavesdropped on a private conversation.'

His audacity amazed her. Surely he should display a modicum of shame at knowing his...his *insults* had been overheard?

Outraged, she swung back at him. 'Is that supposed to make me feel better?'

'It's the truth. Whether it makes you feel better or not is entirely up to you.'

For a long moment their eyes locked, then suddenly a wail sounded upstairs, signalling that Emily had woken.

The sound made Claire jump. She should have been expecting it, but the expected and the unexpected seemed to have merged into one so that she didn't know which was which any more. Brett's arrival had completely destroyed the pattern of her day and now even the familiar had assumed a mantle of unreality.

Confrontation was forgotten as fear nudged her pride and anger aside. What would Brett do when he saw Emily? Would he somehow recognise her as his own?

Don't be ridiculous. She tried to squash the dread rising up inside her. How could Brett possibly recognise her? He'd never even seen her... didn't even know she existed... probably didn't want to know.

Not looking at Brett, she rose from her chair and left the kitchen without saying a word. Upstairs in her bedroom, she picked up the warm, solid body of her daughter and held her close, nuzzling her chin against the dark, downy curls and then watching as the yells of protest turned to smiling gurgles of delight.

That swift ability to switch from wanton demand to compliant amusement still amazed her.

Unconsciously her arms tightened protectively round the baby. Once she had imagined the wonder of sharing the love and pride she felt for her daughter with Brett, but now she could hardly bear the thought of exposing Emily's baby innocence to his hostility.

She stayed in her room as long as possible, postponing the moment when she must go back downstairs, but soon Emily grew restless. She was hungry and wanted her tea.

Slowly Claire made her way back down to the kitchen, taking a deep breath before opening the door and going in. From the security of her mother's arms, Emily's vivid blue eyes, so like Brett's, focused on the dark stranger in its centre.

'Oooh.' She pursed her lips in an experimental greeting, assuming such a comical expression that, had she not been in such a state of frozen paralysis, Claire might have smiled.

But she felt much too tense to smile. Each breath seemed a prolongation of agony as she sought Brett's reaction to his child.

They were so alike: the same dark colouring, the same vivid blue eyes. Surely he must see it too.

Brett had moved to sit down in one of the chairs and now he lounged back in it, observing the two of them with such an odd look on his face that for a moment Claire was sure he did know. But then he looked away and she realised that the fear or perhaps, deep-down, hope of recognition had been totally misplaced. Emily was as much a stranger to him as she was.

Her arms felt numb and, fearful of dropping her daughter, Claire carried Emily over to the high chair and strapped her in, a process which took far longer than it should have done because her fingers were trembling so much.

'Are . . . are you hungry?' she enquired falteringly of Brett as she went over to the stove and began spooning some of the casserole into a bowl for Emily.

He shook his head. 'I'll go down to the pub and get something to eat.'

'Suit yourself.' Claire tilted her chin slightly in defiant acknowledgement, refusing to let him see just how much his deliberate rebuff hurt.

'I always do,' Brett assured her.

It was true, in part. Claire had known it from their first meeting. In his universe, Brett was the sun and other people the satellites who orbited round him. It was a natural order; he accepted it and so did they. Yet she'd never heard him sound so brutally offhand. Not the way he sounded now.

She'd thought she'd known him. Naïvely, as it turned out, she'd believed that in one short week they had discovered an understanding and intimacy which many couples never found in a lifetime together. How wrong she'd been.

Tension clawed at her insides, a tension which she knew must soon transmit itself to Emily, and Claire found herself feverishly hoping that Brett would go to the pub straight away and leave them alone.

Her nerves felt raw as she contemplated the apparently cosy scenario the three of them presented. Mother, father and child! What could be more natural? Yet in the circumstances, what could possibly be more unnatural? Brett had no more idea who she or Emily were than any stranger he might pass on the street.

She was desperate for him to go, for the strained little triangle to be broken, but, for all her desperate wishes, he remained where he was, watching as she began to spoon Emily her tea.

'It's a long time since there was a baby at Sandwood,' he said abruptly. 'Not since Duncan's and Elspeth's kids were younger.'

Duncan had told Claire that Sandwood had been his and Elspeth's holiday home for over twenty years. When their four children were young, they had spent almost every holiday here and had managed in between with just a local woman calling in a couple of times a week to check the house.

As the children had grown older, they had found themselves spending less and less time there, but were reluctant to sell the house they both loved so much. They had discussed the possibility of a housekeeper, but had never got round to doing anything about it, until Claire had telephoned Duncan nearly four months ago and asked him about the possibility of returning to work at Atlas Engineering. She'd hated the idea of leaving Emily while she went back to work, but had seen no other solution to her problems.

By the time they had met, Claire had had other difficulties to contend with. The hostel would only allow her to stay until Emily was three months old and that date was fast approaching. In desperation, she'd poured out her troubles to Duncan, and it was then that he had suggested the housekeeper's job at Sandwood.

It offered a solution to both their problems. Claire would have a home for herself and Emily and a small income too, and the Camerons could be assured that Sandwood would be safe from vandals and burglars.

'She's no trouble,' she said sharply now, defensively interpreting Brett's comment as a complaint. 'She rarely even wakes in the night, but if she does you won't hear her. Your bedroom's a long way from ours. You won't have your sleep disturbed.'

Brett stood up from the table, pushing the chair back on the stone flags with a noisy, grating sound. 'Sleeping's not the problem,' he said tautly. 'It's not the hours when I'm asleep but the hours when I'm awake that my problems start.'

Seconds later the door slammed shut and he was gone, leaving Claire staring after him. She'd never heard Brett sound so bitter and for the first time she realised just how much he hated what had happened to him.

The accident... the months in hospital when he had been dependent on others... the enforced immobility... must all have been torture for a man like him, a man who had probably never known what it was not to feel in total control of his life.

And then, when his physical recovery was complete, to realise that his memory was still incomplete must be sheer hell.

CHAPTER THREE

GOLDEN-HEADED daffodils and pure white snowdrops swayed in their dark, peaty bed beneath the kitchen window, braving the chill of a grey, blustery March day. Claire had watched the buds breaking into flower nearly a fortnight ago and been cheered by the first real sign of spring. Today, though, it wasn't the flowers which drew her eyes as she stood at the old-fashioned porcelain sink. It was Brett.

He was chopping wood, his lithe, muscular body repeatedly stretching and curving as he wielded the axe in rhythmic arcs. The jeans were the same as yesterday but the Aran sweater had been swapped for a blue and grey checked shirt, rolled up now to the elbows.

Claire watched the play of tendons along hard, muscled forearms in reluctant fascination. Whatever course of physiotherapy Brett had undertaken after the accident had successfully resulted in complete physical recovery. There could be no doubt of that. He had been working relentlessly for nearly an hour without a break.

Already a substantial pile of logs was mounting up beside him. They could be burned on the drawing-room fire in the evenings but they weren't really necessary. There was already a plentiful supply of coal and wood in the storage sheds. Claire knew he wasn't doing the chore out of necessity but as an outlet for the pent-up aggression and frustration he was carrying inside him.

His expression was grim and taut. It hadn't relaxed once in the entire time she'd been watching him. What tortuous thoughts were going on inside his head? she wondered. She tried to imagine what it must be like to lose a part of your life, to have no recollection of events or people during a particular time, to meet a blank wall every time you tried to remember them. It must be appalling.

Claire frowned and her fingers stilled on the dishes in the sudsy water. She had the key to that period, part of it at least. And unlocking part of it might unlock the rest of it too. Was it right... fair, even, not to use it?

All night she'd tossed and turned, trying to decide what was the best thing to do, and still come no nearer to an answer.

Perhaps if seeing him again had shown her that her feelings for him were not as strong as time and distance had led her to believe, the answer would have been more easily arrived at. But quite the opposite was true. For the last hour her gaze had been riveted on him, greedily drinking in the sight which had been denied her so long.

Memories, always lurking just beneath the surface of her mind, emerged like sluggish bulbs from their winter rest into bright, dazzling blooms.

'What are you doing here in Sydney?' Brett had asked as they'd danced on that first evening.

Claire had told him about Helen's birthday gift and her decision to spend it on the trip to Australia.

'And has Australia lived up to your expectations?'

Claire nodded. 'It's been wonderful. I love the colours, the wildness, the raw energy, all of it.' It was true, the trip had been wonderful, but nothing she had seen or done so far quite compared with the sensations Brett's touch aroused in her. The blood was soaring through her veins like darting quicksilver, accelerating every pulse-point into overdrive. 'Home's going to seem very dull after this,' she murmured.

'Home?'

'London,' she elaborated, biting back a soft moan as Brett's subtly roving fingers sent a cascade of sensation shooting the full length of her spine.

'You're going back there, then?'

The question surprised her. 'Of course.' Much as she was enjoying her trip, it had never occurred to her not to go back. 'It's where I live.'

'You don't have to live there... You could live anywhere... You could stay in Australia.'

The silky suggestion hung briefly in the air between them as Claire's bemused brain tried to work out whether Brett was in some way propositioning her. Did he mean stay with him in Australia?

He couldn't, she derided her foolish leap of elation. We've only just met.

Still, the suggestion skittled all her attempts at sophisticated conversation and she found herself dazedly on the defensive. 'I...I couldn't...I mean...I...I've got to return to my job.'

'There are other jobs.'

Her heart gave a strange twist. 'But...but I've got to go back. My boss kept my job open. I'd be letting him down if...if I didn't.'

Brett's look was darkly mocking. 'So much loyalty and commitment in one so young! I'm impressed. Just who is this boss capable of inspiring such dedication?'

Fleetingly Claire wondered if Brett was making fun of her. Perhaps she had slightly exaggerated her responsibilities to Duncan Cameron, but he had been very generous all the same.

'Duncan Cameron…chairman of Atlas Engineering.' Brett's hold on her tightened fractionally.

'Do you know him?'

'Mmm, though I haven't seen him for some time.' His reply was non-committal.

Claire didn't find the link particularly surprising. Duncan made regular trips to the company's base in Sydney and had contact with other high-profile business people there. Brett Jarrett must surely move in the same exclusive circles.

'Not only is he keeping my job open for me, he even offered me the use of one of the company apartments in this complex while I'm in Sydney. He's been very kind. I couldn't just not go back,' she explained.

Couldn't she? Not even if a man like Brett Jarrett asked her to stay?

Claire thrust the crazy thought aside. What on earth was she thinking of? She'd hardly known the man five minutes.

The giddy spiralling of her thoughts shocked her. She'd never experienced this sort of wild romanticising before, except in books. But then she'd never met a man like Brett Jarrett before!

'Very kind,' Brett agreed drily. 'Some people might ask why.'

His glance slid over her then in insolent appraisal, leaving Claire in no doubt of his meaning. She jerked back from him, rigid with indignation. 'Can't a boss be kind to an employee without people assuming they're having an affair?' she demanded.

'Not often, no,' Brett informed her, his grip strengthening. 'Few people do kindnesses without an ulterior motive. But I'm willing to grant this case is an exception. I happen to know Duncan's very happily married. I doubt he'd be interested in an affair.'

'And neither would I,' Claire snapped back at him.

'Wouldn't you?' Brett asked with disarming smoothness. Then he smiled, a smile so wickedly seductive that Claire felt her knees turning to jelly.

'What do *you* do?' she asked, steering the subject away from uncharted waters and trying to sound calm as her pulse-rate rocketed alarmingly.

'This and that,' Brett murmured against her ear. 'I'm a sort of trouble-shooter. I travel around a lot.'

The blood seemed to be singing through her veins. 'It sounds exciting.'

'Not really. Tell me more about yourself. Where do you come from? Not London. I can tell that much from your accent.' Brett deftly changed the subject.

'There's not much to tell.'

'Tell me about your family,' he induced softly. 'Have you brothers . . . sisters?'

Claire shook her head. 'I'm an only child.' One mistake had been enough for her parents. They had made sure there weren't any more.

Brett's laugh was warm and husky and scented with wine. 'Were you spoiled?'

It was the stereotyped image of an only child, but there never had been much spoiling during Claire's childhood. By the time she was born, her parents had been in their forties. They were comfortably off financially and quite content with their lifestyle, running a store in a small Yorkshire village. They certainly hadn't bargained on a child coming along and disrupting it.

Claire had never wanted for anything materially, but she'd been aware from a very early age that she wasn't a *wanted* child. She'd been tolerated, but she'd quickly learned that her needs couldn't be allowed to interrupt the smooth-running wheels of her parents' staid lifestyle.

Fortunately she'd had a natural inclination towards solitary pursuits and had spent many an hour on the moors surrounding her home, occupied with a good book or a sketch-pad.

'Absolutely rotten,' she agreed with an attempt at a joke.

Narrowed blue eyes glittered down at her through thick, sooty lashes. 'Why don't I believe you?'

'I...I don't know,' she stammered, not knowing what else to say. Nothing in her experience so far had prepared her for a man like Brett, a man to whom the usual exchange of social niceties was a mere nothing to be brushed aside and dispensed with at will.

'Probably because you don't lie very well. You blush far too easily.'

His thumb came up to brush against the flush of pink which stained her cheeks, deepening it to crimson.

Embarrassed, she dashed his hand away. 'I don't want to lie *well*,' she informed him, piqued. 'It's not an accomplishment I wish to acquire.'

He laughed then, a low, sexy sound, throwing back his head and exposing the hard angles of his jawline.

'Did I make it sound like a complaint? I'm sorry. It was intended as a compliment.'

The slashing smile and the swift, unexpected apology were as intriguing as they were confusing and, contrarily, Claire felt herself slipping deeper under Brett's spell.

Afterwards he walked her to her apartment. She thought he might ask if he could come in and spent the five-minute journey agonising over what she would say if he did. But in fact Brett merely kissed her briefly on the cheek and walked away.

If his coolness was a ploy to whet her appetite, it worked. Convinced she would never see him again, Claire went straight to bed and wept.

The next morning, when the phone in her apartment rang and it was Brett, sheer, unadulterated relief flooded through her and, with almost desperate eagerness, she agreed to another meeting.

'Huh hmm.'

The sound was intrusive and at the same time curiously reminiscent.

Horrified, Claire swung round to find Brett standing in the kitchen doorway, Emily in his arms.

The sight of them together wrenched at her heart and for a moment she could only stare at them dazedly. They were so different; a tall, lean, powerful male holding a small baby. So dissimilar and yet so alike because, although neither of them realised it, they were father and daughter.

Emily was too young to understand, but was it fair, right even, to keep the knowledge of that relationship from Brett?

Reassured by her mother's presence, Emily relaxed into his arms, turning to examine him intently, her chubby baby fingers moving to explore the growth of black stubble on his jawline.

She hadn't come into contact with many men and Brett's roughened skin, where he hadn't bothered to shave that morning, was a source of curiosity for her.

Claire dashed her hands against a towel and stepped forward, shocked to discover that her reverie had been so deep that she hadn't even been aware that Brett had stopped working and had moved out of sight. She wondered if he had realised, from her stance by the window, that she had been watching him.

'What's the matter?' she began, automatically reaching forward to take Emily from him. Fleetingly their fingers touched and Claire felt the scorching shock of the contact travel all the way up her arm.

'She woke up and was yelling—very loudly,' Brett said, eyes narrowing briefly as he handed the child over.

Emily had been asleep in her pram, sheltered by the porch. Normally Claire always kept an ear open for her. Now she felt horribly guilty that she hadn't heard her daughter's cries. She'd been too absorbed in memories of that first meeting with Brett. 'You should have called me. I would have got her,' she said, self-recrimination making her response harsher than she intended.

'I'm quite capable of picking up a baby. What did you think I was going to do? Drop her?' Brett retorted, hands dropping to rest on denim-clad hips as he surveyed her across the room.

'No, I——'

'I waited a few minutes expecting you to come. In the end her yells were getting louder and louder so it seemed easier to pick her up myself.'

Claire turned, allowing a swath of silvery blonde hair to swing across her face and screen the tell-tale blush which flooded her cheeks. Brett thought she was angry with him when in fact she was angry with herself. She was shocked too by the emotional tug of painful pleasure seeing him and Emily together had provoked.

She'd pictured them together often in her mind, but the reality was a thousand times more poignant.

'I'm sorry if she interrupted you,' she murmured in a more conciliatory tone.

'I was only chopping wood, for God's sake, not preparing a speech for the United Nations,' Brett gibed, his mood evidently no less terse than it had been on the previous night. 'I needed a drink anyway. It's thirsty work.' And he moved to fill a glass at the sink.

Moments later he leaned back against the white porcelain and took a gulp of the icy cold spring water. Claire watched as the tanned column of his throat flexed in muscular contractions.

'She's not very like you, is she?' he said, tilting his glass to indicate Emily.

Claire frowned. 'In what way?'

'Colouring. You're very blonde and she's very dark.'

'She's more like her father.' The come-back was swift and spontaneous and not at all what she had intended to say.

Why had she said it? Had she already, deep down, reached a decision? She wanted Brett to know the truth, but hadn't the grit to come right out with it. Was she instead playing psychological games, deliberately laying down clues in the hope that he would pick up on them?

'There is a father, then?'

What on earth did he mean by that? 'Of course Emily has a father,' she retorted, confused.

Brett's mouth thinned cynically. 'I didn't just mean in the biological sense. A single act of intercourse hardly counts as taking on the responsibilities of fatherhood. I meant, one who's still around... involved. Duncan said you never mentioned him. He presumed the relationship must be over.'

So Duncan had surmised that much at least. She'd been grateful that he'd asked so few questions, but she supposed it was unreasonable to imagine that he wouldn't have made some conjectures about her condition and the circumstances of Emily's conception. 'Duncan never said anything to me.'

'Duncan's too tactful to say anything,' Brett informed her drily. 'He was worried about upsetting you.'

'And you're not, I suppose?' she said tautly.

Brett shrugged, the checked material of his shirt rising over the broad arc of his shoulders. 'I've never considered reticence a particular virtue. Far more misunderstandings are caused by *not* asking what you want to know.'

'And possibly far more acrimony by not getting the answers you want to hear.'

'That's the chance you have to take.'

No doubt it was a chance Brett was always prepared to take. Claire didn't know that she possessed his audacity. 'Why should you want to know about Emily's father anyway?' With difficulty she kept her voice neutral, trying not to let it sound as if the answer could bring her world tumbling down around her shoulders.

Brett took another swig of the crystal-clear water. 'Curiosity, I suppose. Your daughter can't be very old... What is she? Six or seven months? Even in this day and age, it's somewhat unusual for both parents not still to be around at that stage.'

So it was only curiosity and not a deeper motive which had prompted the enquiry. Perhaps that should have brought relief, but perversely she felt disappointed... thwarted.

Damn Brett Jarrett! Surely she and Emily deserved a little more than idle curiosity from him?

'Not so unusual,' she murmured tautly.

'So the relationship is over, then?'

From the first moment that she'd met him, Claire had known that Brett was direct. There was no room in his life for the tentative overtures most people made in their dealings with others. If he wanted something, no one was left in any doubt of his intention to get it. How they dealt with that determination was their problem, not his.

Fifteen months ago, she had been dazed, and not a little flattered, by his uninhibited pursuit of her. She had never met a man like him before and that explicit candour had been no small part of his appeal.

Now she found it threatening. She was walking on quicksand with no idea where his questions, or her answers, might be leading her.

'Y...yes,' she admitted. It was the truth after all. How could you describe a relationship where one party didn't even remember the other as anything but over?

'You must still have some contact with him, though?'

'Why must I?' Ragged nerves forced out the terse demand. 'I told you. The relationship is over.'

Vivid blue eyes narrowed. 'What about maintenance... child support? Don't you even receive any money from him?'

A wild, rapid pulse beat in Claire's throat and a roaring panic filled her ears. She was edging closer and closer to the edge of a waterfall. Did she dig her heels in now or carry on and risk being dragged over the edge?

Of course she could always tell Brett to mind his own business. He had no right to fire this stream of questions at her simply to satisfy his idle curiosity, but she was aware of a curious kind of compulsive need to tell him the truth.

'I...no. Our relationship was over before I even realised I was pregnant. He doesn't know about Emily.'

Brett made a contemptuous sound somewhere deep in his throat. 'He doesn't know? What sort of selfish feminist thinking is that? Why the hell didn't you tell him? Doesn't he have a right to know about the existence of his child?'

Claire's eyes blazed. 'It's not any kind of feminist thinking. It's just the way it is. I don't like it any more than you do.'

'Yet you've done nothing to change it.'

Already knowing she'd admitted too much, Claire crouched low to set Emily down on a rug on the floor and made a great play of scattering some coloured bricks in front of her. She was trembling all over. 'It...it's difficult.'

'Of course it's difficult but that doesn't mean it shouldn't be done.'

'He...he lives abroad.'

'So? Postal services do operate in countries other than England.'

His sarcasm was like a whiplash on raw flesh. 'If you must know, I did write but he didn't reply.'

Not he, *you*. She wanted to cry the amendment aloud, sickened by the subterfuge. The strain of keeping silent was like a burning, over-wound spring inside her.

There was a brief silence and then Brett frowned. 'Are you sure your letters got through?'

'Of course I'm sure.'

Another strained silence. 'Then it would seem you're right.' His mouth twisted. 'Perhaps he isn't interested.'

She registered the small victory without any sense of triumph for, whether Brett realised it or not, he was admitting his own lack of interest.

A shudder of mortification gripped her. Why was she so shocked? Brett had lied to her, by omission if not by word, and abandoned her when she'd most needed him. Why should the confirmation of this last betrayal be so piercing?

Brett set his glass down with a dull thud. 'I don't understand how anyone, a man or woman, can turn their back on their own flesh and blood.' Bitterness tugged at the hard edges of his mouth, hinting at some private grievance known only to himself.

Claire stared at him, incredulity stamped on her delicate features. He sounded disgusted, yet wasn't that precisely what Brett had done, turned his back on her and Emily?

Had the accident wrought more changes than perhaps even Brett realised? Had his attitudes changed? Was he now prepared to accept responsibilities he hadn't been prepared to face a year ago?

Her mind revolved in frantic circles. What if she were to tell Brett the truth right now? Dared she risk it?

'You haven't any children, then?' she asked with a boldness she was far from feeling.

'No.' The denial was stark and conclusive.

For a moment her courage wavered. 'You…you sound very positive.'

A muscle twitched along Brett's jaw and his mouth curved drily. 'I am. I have no hang-ups about using contraception, I can assure you.'

Colour flooded Claire's cheeks as Brett's assertion brought back memories she was barely able to confront right now.

What he said was true enough, she acknowledged painfully. She was the one who had been irresponsible about birth control, not he.

What had happened on that last night in Sydney hadn't been planned, certainly not by her.

Unsure how to tell Brett that she was a virgin, she had delayed telling him until it was too late. Brought to a pitch of passion and desire beyond her wildest dreams, she had passed the point of considering any future consequences of their actions, and when Brett had whispered, 'Is it OK to go further?' she had nodded and whispered 'yes', over and over again. In her naïveté she had not realised that he had been subtly asking if she was protected, not referring to her sexual arousal.

The moment of realisation had come too late for either of them to do anything about it. Claire had clenched briefly in response to stabbing pain, momentarily retreating from the brink of paradise. But almost in the space of her heartbeat her aroused body had urged her back, irresistibly tugging her towards the release it sought, until she had tumbled helplessly into wave after wave of ecstasy.

Moments later, Brett's roughly groaned question, 'Why the hell didn't you tell me you were a virgin?' had jarred the delightfully blurred edges of her consciousness.

Her eyes had fluttered open to encounter his black-fringed gaze staring down at her. 'D-does it matter?'

'It could.'

She'd frowned then, unable to reconcile that brief, terse statement with the gloriously fierce lovemaking which had preceded it. Heat had suddenly evaporated from her body. 'H-how?'

'It's bloody irresponsible, that's how. You're not protected at all, are you?'

With the weight of his body still on hers, there had been no escape, no evasion, only the dark, brooding intensity of his eyes on hers. In a sudden rush of lucidity, Claire had realised that earlier Brett had been referring to contraception. Her heart had hammered painfully against her chest as she had realised how naïvely irresponsible she'd been.

Her stricken look had given Brett his answer and he had rolled off her then, muttering an expletive under his breath.

In an agony of pain, Claire had clutched the sheet to her, hardly able to believe that the exquisite beauty of only a few minutes before had so quickly dissipated. A tear had clung precariously to her lower lashes, wobbled briefly, and then slid down her cheek.

Seeing it, Brett had crushed her against him. 'Don't cry,' he'd murmured roughly.

'I'm sorry.'

'I just never suspected...' His arms had tightened round her, drawing her against the solid wall of his chest, so close that she had been able to feel the deep, steady rhythm of his heartbeat. 'Don't worry. It was a mistake... only one... It won't happen again.'

When they had made love the second time, *he* had made sure they used contraception.

One mistake! It was the wrong moment for that bittersweet memory to surface. It badly eroded the courage which had inspired her feat of daring in broaching the subject at all.

Her throat felt parched and she could barely utter the question she needed to ask. 'Then... then you're quite sure you don't have a child whose existence you're unaware of?'

'Quite sure.'

Claire met the categorical denial on a wave of misery. He sounded so sure. How was she ever going to be able to tell him the truth?

If his memory didn't return naturally, then he would never remember her. Even if she told him that Emily was his, he wouldn't believe her.

Oh, yes, there were various tests that could prove paternity, she knew that, but she didn't want that. She wanted Brett to know the truth in his heart, not because it was printed on a piece of paper.

His glance went fleetingly to Emily as she lay on her stomach, tiny fists reaching out to try to grab the coloured bricks which rested just outside her grasp.

'I wouldn't be irresponsible enough to allow a child of mine to be born outside a stable relationship. A child needs that security.'

The terse declaration brought a second shock wave to Claire's already fragile composure. She had never guessed he held such strong views on parenthood.

How could she? One brief week's relationship could not provide a catalogue of attitudes, and his silence in the face of her letters had led her to believe his interest in parenthood was perfunctory to say the least.

'Surely what a child needs most is love?' she suggested tautly. Eighteen months ago she would have endorsed his views one hundred per cent, supremely confident that the single-parent scenario would never apply to her. But now her own experiences had taught her not to be quite so intransigent on the subject.

'A child needs security, emotional and physical,' Brett insisted. 'And one parent cannot easily provide both.'

Claire frowned, sensing the underlying criticism of her own situation. 'Not easily, maybe, but it's not impossible.'

'Without adequate means of financial support, I believe it is. Look at your own circumstances. Duncan told me you were desperate to get this job. You had no home, no income. How can you raise a child like that?'

'You're only talking about material things,' Claire protested, a little desperately. 'Just because you grew up surrounded by wealth, you think it's essential to a child's well-being. It isn't.'

Brett's black brows snapped together. 'Of course wealth isn't essential. I'm not talking about luxuries; I'm talking about necessities. As she gets older, how are you going to provide for her?'

'I'll work. I'll manage,' Claire insisted. Her nails were grooving painful arcs into the palms of her clenched fists.

'Will you? Juggling a full-time job, a home and a child?'

'Lots of single parents do it.'

'Yes, and lots of children are scarred for life as a result.'

A fist of fear tightened round Claire's heart, making the muscles work overtime in frantic reaction as an appalling prospect occurred to her. Was it possible that Brett might try to take Emily from her if he knew the truth? Did he consider her an unfit mother, unfit to bring up any child, let alone *his*?

And what view might a court take? She had nothing. No family support, no home, no proper income. Brett had everything that she lacked in abundance.

Brett's refusal to respond to her letters had made it clear that he had no interest in continuing his relationship with her, but perhaps he really hadn't understood the confused messages they contained. Perhaps he hadn't realised she was pregnant. What if he should want to acknowledge his child after all, and not just to be an absentee father but the custodial parent?

'It's none of my business, of course, but if I were you I'd try to contact the father again. At the very least he should make some financial contribution to his child's welfare.'

Claire watched, white-faced, as he left the room, absorbing the noise of the door slamming shut without reaction. She felt numb with shock.

'It's none of my business.' The bitter irony of that statement brought its own despondency.

It had everything to do with Brett, but how would she ever dare to tell him now?

CHAPTER FOUR

CLAIRE stared gloomily into her coffee-cup. She'd come into Keswick on the pretext of doing the weekly grocery shop, but in fact she'd wanted to phone Helen in private. She couldn't be sure that any calls she made from the house wouldn't be overheard by Brett.

Tossing and turning in her bed last night, she had gone over and over what Brett had said, trying to understand what it meant, trying to work out how he would react if he knew the truth about Emily.

Would he regret what had happened and offer her support? Or would he blame her in some way and try to take Emily away from her?

She didn't know the answer and because of that she realised that she simply couldn't risk him finding out the truth. The consequences were too terrible to contemplate.

Painful though the prospect of leaving him again was, she had reached the conclusion that there was only one option open to her. For Emily's sake, she had to get away, and the only place she could go was Helen's.

It was far from ideal; the small cottage in Cornwall accommodated one comfortably, two at a squeeze. Three, even when one of them was a baby, would mean that the walls were bursting at the seams.

The tiny whitewashed cottage with its minute garden, near Tintagel, was a deliberate choice of base on Helen's part. Since she spent much of her time abroad, she saw no point in wasting money on maintaining a large, empty property and, despite the amount of travelling she did, she'd acquired few belongings on the way. Collecting experiences was far more important to her than collecting possessions.

She had been a wonderful source of support during Claire's pregnancy. She'd neither asked questions nor made judgements but had simply offered help and a home when Claire had had nowhere else to go. Claire had stayed with her almost until Emily was born. Helen had wanted her to stay longer, but Claire had known the strain a baby's arrival would make on the already cramped living arrangements and on an elderly lady not accustomed to children.

Thus she had been determined to manage independently. She'd spent a couple of months in a hostel in London and then, after meeting Duncan, come to Sandwood. Everything had seemed to be working out well, but yesterday the fragile structure of her new life had collapsed and this morning Claire knew she had no option but to phone Helen and encroach on her hospitality once again.

Helen had been delighted to hear from her. As usual, her conversation had shot off at several different tangents all at once. 'Darling, how are you? And Emily? I'm so glad I've been able to speak to you. I lost your telephone number, you know. You'll never guess—I'm off to Brazil tomorrow with Colonel Anderson and his wife...remember them?'

To Claire, Helen's impending trip had seemed a godsend. For once the fates were working in her favour.

If Helen was away, she needn't worry about the inconvenience she and Emily would cause in going to stay.

'Will you be leaving the cottage empty?' she'd enquired casually.

A soft chuckle had sounded down the line. 'Only in a manner of speaking. It's already full of builders.'

'Builders?'

'Yes, I'm afraid all the structural timbers need replacing... Like me, the old place is getting rather ancient... and since it's going to be uninhabitable for quite some time it's best to get the job done while I'm out of the country.'

Claire had tried to stifle her gasp of dismay at learning that her only bolt-hole was closed. 'That... that sounds like a good idea.'

Helen had sighed. 'I suppose so. Though I don't like to think of the poor old place being ripped apart. Still, in a few months it'll be as good as new, so they tell me. You'll have to come and see it when it's all spruced up.'

Claire had known she couldn't burden her aunt with her own problems or spoil her forthcoming trip, so she had forced a lighter note into her voice. 'That would be lovely. I'll look forward to it.'

Inwardly, though, she had shivered. A few months' time! By then it might well be too late, she had thought desolately as she'd set the receiver back in its cradle.

Numbly she'd made her way to the tea-rooms on Keswick's main street and, after manoeuvring a sleeping Emily and her buggy into a corner, had sat down at one of the small round tables and ordered coffee.

Now though the coffee was cold and bitter and she was still no nearer to finding any solution to her problems.

Common sense told her that, as an unmarried father, Brett would have few rights in the eyes of a British court. But what about in the eyes of an Australian court? If he should *snatch* Emily and take her back to Australia, how would she fare trying to fight for custody on the other side of the world?

Such things did happen. She'd read about them in newspapers and magazines. Human-interest stories! Oh, yes! They were *interesting* while they were happening to someone else. It was an entirely different matter when they happened to you!

She felt as if she was holding a time bomb in her hands. 'Given time, his memory should return naturally,' Duncan had told her. Now it seemed she had no choice but to pray that it didn't.

Impossible though it seemed, she had no choice but to return to Sandwood and try to get through the daily agony of being so close to Brett and the daily dread of his finding out the truth.

There had been heavy rains recently and as she drove out of Keswick and back up the valley streaming jets of water gushed down from the fells, causing small rivulets to form by the side of the road. A pale sun shone tentatively in the sky, its rays glancing off the temporary falls in dazzling kaleidoscopes of colour.

Another time, Claire would have longed to capture the effect on canvas, but today she was too beset by worries to spare the scenic beauty surrounding her more than a cursory glance. She gazed across at her daughter.

Whatever happens, I won't let him take you from me, she vowed.

Just seeing Brett's Range Rover parked in the drive when she arrived back at the house caused her heart to thump more vigorously, but she quickly realised he wasn't at home.

The day was bright and clear and she guessed he'd gone for a walk. A good, long one, she hoped. When he wasn't around, it was easier to pretend that the last few days had never happened and that she and Emily were still living here alone.

Like the proverbial ostrich, she wanted to put her head in the sand and pretend none of this was happening. Coward! she chided herself. What was the point of make-believe when she had to deal with reality?

After unpacking the shopping, Claire gave Emily her lunch then set her outside in her pram for her afternoon nap. The sun's first tentative rays had strengthened and now it was quite warm outdoors, the first real spring day.

The hotels and shopkeepers will be pleased if this keeps up, she thought idly. Easter weekend was fast approaching and good weather always brought more visitors to the area.

Back in the kitchen she felt unusually restless and confined. She picked up the newspaper she'd bought in town but the words blurred into a grey and white jumble. How could she possibly concentrate on world affairs when her own life was so out of kilter?

Impatiently she tossed it aside and went to stand at the kitchen window, gazing out at the distant mountaintops with yearning, wishing she could be on them.

Many a time as a child she had escaped on to the Yorkshire Moors near her home, walking for miles to exorcise the frustrations and hurt which parental lack of warmth had generated. Today she longed to do the same, but of course she couldn't leave Emily.

Instead she went outside, passing through the gardens and then into the orchard turned golden with its yellow carpet of dancing daffodils.

Sandwood was situated halfway up a rise and its grounds offered wonderful views over Derwentwater, stretching out like a sheet of jagged pewter in the valley below. Around and above, grey slate peaks dipped and rose in angular configurations which punctured the skyline, culminating in the white-tipped peak of Skiddaw, still bearing its winter gown of snow.

Claire leaned against the fence, careful to avoid the thick clusters of dazzling white snowdrops which fluttered round her ankles, feeling the breeze ruffle her hair and froth the silky blonde strands into tousled disarray.

Briefly she closed her eyes, listening to the sweet, liquid song of a skylark as it rose in the sky and drawing gulps of bracken-scented air into her lungs, wishing its raw freshness could expunge all her anxieties.

'Are you all right?'

Two shocked pools of violet flew open to find Brett standing just feet away from her.

He had been walking, she saw from his boots, probably on Derwent Fells at the back of the house. The wind up there had whipped his hair into a dark halo around his head and his eyes seemed to have absorbed the rich blue of the deepest mountain tarns. His face was all hard angles and curves, as rugged as the granite monoliths which surrounded them.

He took another step towards her and the impact of his nearness hit her in wave after giddy wave as a musky, male smell, scented with bracken and heather, invaded her nostrils.

'Y-yes.'

'You looked pensive.'

'Did I?'

They were staring at each other, their faces only inches apart, eyes threaded by an invisible silk.

Claire could feel the powerful thudding of her heartbeat, the blood moving in quickened response through her veins, the warm ache in the pit of her stomach.

For one crazy, agonising moment she thought he was going to kiss her and knew that if he did she would do nothing to prevent it, but then he turned to stare out over the lake, his expression as dark and brooding as its deep waters.

'You know, when I saw you standing there, you reminded me of someone...' he said, not looking at her. 'Either that or I've met you before.'

Every ounce of breath seemed to leave Claire's lungs and a terrible fear filled the vacuum created.

When she offered no response, Brett turned back to face her. 'Have you ever been to Australia?'

Her bloodflow accelerated into overdrive, powered by panic now, not sexual arousal. He knows! A mallet blow hammered home the awful thought.

'No!' She lied instinctively and immediately.

Brett's eyes narrowed. 'You're sure?' Then he frowned. 'No! Scrap that. It's a stupid question. Of course you're sure. You'd know if you'd been to Australia, wouldn't you?'

The lie had been a little too stark and defensive to be wholly convincing, but Brett appeared to accept it, Claire noted with sick relief. Probably because his memories, if they were what had triggered the question, were subconscious ones, too vague and tenuous for him to credit as real.

But how long before they took a more solid form and he recognised them for the truth they were? Surely it could only be a matter of time?

She was playing with fire and every lie she uttered was feeding the flames. If Brett did discover the truth, he would be furious. He would hate her for deceiving him further when she could have enlightened him. God knew what form his revenge might take. She shivered.

Brett watched her reaction with narrowed eyes. 'Cold?'

Claire nodded. 'I think I'll get back to the house.'

'I'll come too. I've walked enough for today.'

To Claire's dismay, Brett fell into step beside her as she headed back up the orchard. He even waited while she paused to check the pram, but Emily was sleeping peacefully and she had little choice but to follow him into the kitchen.

Once there, Brett sat down on one of the chairs and began taking off his boots while Claire stood awkwardly in the doorway.

'Aren't you going to come in?' he demanded, lifting his head to look at her when she remained where she was.

He thinks I'm behaving oddly, she thought on a wave of desperation and wished her acting abilities weren't so abysmally feeble.

But it was no use. She was no good at subterfuge. Even a white lie could make her blush and stammer like a schoolgirl. Duplicity on this scale was quite beyond her power to handle.

'No, I—I've got a few chores to do upstairs,' she muttered and then fled up the stairs.

Where will all the lies end? she wondered wretchedly, sinking down on to her bed.

It was amazing what scale of emotions one human being could awaken in another, she thought. Once Brett had lifted her to the heights of ecstasy; she had never felt more alive in all her life than she had during that week in Sydney with him.

Raised in a home where any display of emotion was regarded as suspect, Claire had learned from an early age to curb any show of feelings which broke through the barrier of inhibition and restraint set by her parents.

Thus she had learned that to be too overtly enthusiastic or eager about anything was certain to result in that activity being severely limited or even banned. Excitement was not a tendency to be encouraged.

Likewise tears did not produce sympathy but disapproval, laughter not amusement but censure, defiance not reasoning but punishment.

If it had not been for Helen, Claire thought she would have grown up believing that such repressive behaviour was entirely normal. Friendships with other children were not encouraged—their flat above the shop was not suitable for children's games, her parents told her—and so Claire had little experience to compare her own with.

Helen's occasional visits, bringing laughter and vitality into the colourless Seymour household, were almost her only proof that not everyone lived by the same narrow conventions as her parents. But it was Brett who had truly shown her how rich human expression could be.

He was so gloriously uninhibited in everything he did. He said what he thought, did what he chose, asked what he wanted to know. And, unlike many powerful men, he was not afraid to encourage others to do the same.

Such lack of constraint had at first shocked Claire and then delighted her. She had revelled in it, believing—falsely, as events showed—that it was tempered by an innate sense of justice which prohibited deliberate hurt or cruelty.

She lay on the bed and closed her eyes, transported back to one gloriously hot afternoon on Bondi Beach. The sun had been a blazing orb of shimmering orange in a brilliant, delphineum-blue sky, the sand warm and golden beneath her.

After a couple of hours' swimming and surfing, she and Brett had found a quiet corner of the beach and gone to lie down for a rest.

Eyes closed and pleasantly drowsy, Claire had been distantly aware of Brett leaning across her, his powerful torso casting a shadow over the bare skin of her abdomen between the bikini top and bottom. His fingers had gently tangled in her hair, drawing her mouth to his, licking the salt from her lips.

His touch had been deliberately tantalising, a velvet promise which made her lips part softly in anticipation.

'You taste of the sea,' he murmured as his fingers traced the delicate curve of her jawline.

'Fishy?' Claire tried to hide her arousal in mock-pique.

Brett shook his head, smiling. 'The way I imagine a mermaid would taste. A mermaid with an exquisite body.'

'But no legs,' Claire murmured ruefully.

'Mmm.' Brett's gaze slid down to the golden length of her slender thighs. 'That would be a loss, I agree. But at least I wouldn't have to chase her far.'

'You would in the sea.'

'But I intend to keep her on land.'

Trailing fingers swept across her midriff, drawing a ball of fire in their wake. A sweet-sharp sensation of desire clenched her stomach and hope leapt inside her. Did Brett know what he did to her when he spoke like that? she wondered. Did he realise the dreams he helped to weave?

'Is there anyone waiting for you in England when you go back?' he demanded huskily.

Their eyes met briefly and Claire knew he was re-ferring to another man. She stared into jet-black pupils and shook her head. 'No one.'

His mouth lowered to the hollow at the base of her throat. 'I'm glad,' he murmured against her skin.

She wanted to tell him that there had never been anyone, that no man had ever aroused the responses he did, but the words caught in her throat as the warm moistness of Brett's tongue sent a trail of pleasure skimming over the curve of her shoulder.

She closed her eyes, as wave after wave of pleasure rippled across her skin, like sea water lapping on golden sand.

'Do you... I mean... is there anyone special... a woman?' she asked hesitantly, not sure if she could really bear to hear the answer.

A fleeting shadow darkened Brett's eyes and he frowned.

Instantly Claire regretted the impulsive urge which had prompted the question. Instincts bred into her from childhood triggered an apology for daring to venture such an enquiry.

'I'm sorry. It doesn't matter. I shouldn't have asked,' she said quickly.

'Why shouldn't you?' Brett asked quietly, eyes scanning her anxious features. 'You have as much right to ask as I did.'

'I thought you looked... annoyed.'

His mouth curved slightly. 'Even if I had, that's no reason for you to apologise. In fact you should have been bloody furious with me. What sort of chauvinist would I be if I believed I was entitled to ask you about your relationships with other men but that it shouldn't work the other way round?'

Rationally she had agreed with him, but, brought up in a household where any anger or displeasure on the part of her parents had been invariably presented as *her* fault, Claire had been conditioned to believe that applied to everyone.

At that moment she had fallen a little deeper in love with him and, caught up in the magic of his lovemaking, it hadn't been until later, much later, that she had realised he hadn't answered her question.

Now the distant sound of the telephone ringing down in the kitchen penetrated her reverie. She listened for a few minutes, heard Brett answer it, and then let out a sigh of relief as she guessed it must be for him.

His, 'Claire—telephone,' some minutes later made her jump up startled from the bed.

'It's Duncan,' Brett informed her drily, handing her the receiver as she entered the kitchen. 'He wants to talk to you himself, just to check I haven't murdered you.'

Claire shot him a surprised look and then lifted the receiver to her ear. 'Duncan?'

'Hello, Claire, I just wanted to have a word and make sure everything was all right.'

'Everything's fine,' Claire assured him quickly, conscious of Brett sitting only a few feet away from her and listening to every word she said.

Duncan cleared his throat. 'I—er—I didn't just mean with the house; I meant between you and Brett. Are you getting on OK?'

'Fine,' Claire lied brightly.

'You're sure he's not giving you a hard time?'

If she hadn't felt like a coiled spring inside, Claire might have laughed. *Hard time*? That was an understatement! He was making her life impossible.

'No, of course not.' She numbly played out the rhetoric of untruths.

'That's all right, then.' Duncan sounded relieved. 'Elspeth was worried about you. She insisted I phone and check. I told her she was probably over-reacting.'

Would Elspeth have been as convinced by those brief assurances as Duncan had been? Claire wondered. Duncan was a kind man, but he didn't like scratching beneath the surface of human behaviour, preferring to see what he wanted to see rather than a possibly darker reality. Elspeth was more perceptive.

A few minutes later, she settled the receiver back in its cradle and then hugged her arms to her in an unconsciously protective posture.

Brett was lounging back in one of the chairs by the table, one leg resting at right angles on the other. He'd not budged throughout the exchange. In dark jeans and a black sweater, he looked for all the world like a rather large, rather dangerous cat making itself at home in the kitchen.

'Duncan seemed to think I might have been upsetting you. Have I?' he enquired coolly, with about as much show of concern as a predatory cat displayed for a mouse it was about to jump on.

His darkly mocking tone annoyed her. 'Would it really matter to you if you had?' she demanded.

'It might.'

'But then again it might not?' she retorted.

He shrugged. 'Believe it or not, I don't go out of my way to upset people, but I don't walk on eggshells trying to avoid it either. If I've said or done something to rattle you, tell me. At least we can talk about it.'

'Said or done something?' Everything he said, everything he did, disturbed her. His being here at all appalled her. Could they talk about that? Of course they couldn't.

Her slender shoulders lifted in a briefly dismissive gesture. 'You haven't upset me. Why should you? After all, we're ... we're virtually strangers.'

Why had she said that? Did she hope that if she used the word 'strangers' often enough Brett would be convinced of its truth?

If that was the case, her reasoning wasn't very sound. Her insistence was just as likely to arouse his suspicions.

As if to prove that very point, Brett's eyes narrowed and he shook his head. 'Yet I still have the strangest feeling I know you from somewhere.'

Claire's heart flipped a somersault. 'You don't.'

'You're very positive.'

'I—I'd know you...remember you if we'd met before.' Every word she uttered was sinking her deeper into a mire of her own making, yet not of her own wishing.

Brett looked thoughtful. 'Have you ever done any modelling?'

'That's got to be a joke.' Claire gave a nervous laugh. 'I'd need the aid of a step-ladder to make it as a model.'

At five feet four inches, she was of average height, but nowhere near tall enough to be mistaken for a mannequin.

But Brett continued to stare at her. 'I meant photographic modelling. Magazine shots... You're really very lovely.'

Scarlet invaded Claire's cheeks and embarrassed heat spread through her body. 'Don't make fun of me,' she retorted angrily. 'If that's your idea of a joke it's not very amusing.'

'Why should it be a joke? Why should it be anything except the truth? Or do compliments offend you?' Brett shot back.

Once he'd told her that he found her beautiful and she'd accepted it. Not because she thought it was really true, but because she'd believed it was his perception of her. Beauty is in the eye of the beholder, as the proverb went.

She'd fallen for it once but she wasn't about to fall for it again! Outrage stiffened her body.

'Yes, when they're so obviously insincere. Save those kind of blandishments for your women friends. I'm not interested in them.'

Brett's look was furious. 'My God! That's quite some chip you've got on your shoulder, lady. It's almost the size of a tree trunk. One man lets you down and we're all tarred with the same brush, is that it? What the hell did you think I was trying to do? Seduce you?'

Claire was shaking. 'I don't care what you were trying to do. I just want to make it clear that I'm not interested in your lies.'

Brett moved so quickly that Claire barely had time to register what he was doing. He leapt up from his chair, came and grabbed her shoulders, and twisted her round to face the mirror. 'What do you see?' he demanded roughly.

She tried to twist away, but he wouldn't let her. His hands bit painful grooves into her shoulders. 'Look at yourself,' he insisted, forcing her to stare at her reflection. 'Now what do you see?'

Her cheeks were flushed and her eyes bright with anger so that their shade had deepened to the colour of spring pansies. She hadn't bothered combing her hair since coming in and it billowed in a silky golden mass around the delicate structure of her face. The pink mouth which could curve with laughter was tight now with temper.

'Me, of course,' she said through gritted teeth.

'And?'

'And nothing.'

Brett shook her. 'Don't be so bloody perverse. Look at yourself. You're a beautiful woman. Why are you too scared or too proud to admit it?'

Suddenly, to her horror, Claire felt a lump rise in her throat, and hot, scalding tears began to slide down her cheeks.

Brett stared at her reflection in the mirror and then swore under his breath. 'God, I'm sorry,' he murmured softly. 'That got out of hand.' And the next moment he was hauling her round to face him and Claire could do nothing but bury her head into the warm roughness of his jumper and bawl her eyes out.

She had no idea how long they stood there. Once she started crying her tears just wouldn't stop. It was as if the flow had been dammed for weeks and had just broken violently through the barrage. Great sobs jerked her body uncontrollably.

Brett didn't seem to mind; he just held her close, stroking her hair and whispering soothing words, the way he might have done to a distressed child.

Afterwards, when her sobs had subsided, he seemed in no rush to let her go, cradling her body against his until a different kind of tension came between them.

Claire felt it first, or at least she thought she did, a peculiar quickening of the pulse and at the same time a strange lethargy creeping through her body. She wanted to pull away from Brett and couldn't. She curved against him, feeling the hardness of packed muscles against her limbs.

Brett bent his head and his mouth brushed against her forehead, teasing back the disarray of silky strands of hair, and then dropped lower to skim her eyelids.

The sensation of his tongue brushing over her damp lids was pleasant and yet not pleasant. Too disturbing to be pleasant, it sent an involuntary shudder through her body.

And when his mouth dropped lower to graze her cheeks and then her lips, she tilted her head towards him, lifting her mouth to his.

His tongue traced the full curve of her lower lip, making it tremble and part beneath his probing touch. Claire was filled with an unbearable hunger. Her arms coiled round Brett's neck, drawing him closer, deepening the kiss until their tongues twined together in passionate exploration.

She had ached for this, wanted it for so long; a soft moan escaped her lips with the unbearable sweetness of the moment.

That muted sound of pleasure brought her to her senses. Oh, God! How could she? How could she have allowed this to happen? A horrible guilt overwhelmed her and she jerked violently away from Brett. 'That shouldn't have happened,' she lashed out at him, appalled at what she'd done.

Frowning, he let her go then stared at her with a strange expression on his face. 'No... no, it shouldn't,' he agreed slowly at last, watching her through narrowed eyes as though trying to pin down some distant and elusive memory.

Then he shook his head and shrugged. 'No, it shouldn't,' he repeated, more forcefully. His mouth thinned. 'But let's not make some big deal out of it, huh? You enjoyed it; I enjoyed it. Let's just forget it.'

Forget it! She wanted to scream out loud or hit him. Anything to get rid of the violent frustration inside her bursting to get out. 'Forget it! Is that all you can say?' she demanded shrilly.

Brett's hands dropped to his hips and his eyes glittered angrily. 'For God's sake! It was just a kiss. There's no need to make such a big deal of it.'

'Just a kiss'! Was that all it was? She'd been buffeted by an earthquake zone and he called it 'just a kiss'. She clasped her arms tightly round her body to stop herself doing something savage and aggressive. 'Well, I don't want your kisses,' she told him furiously.

Yet another lie. She needed his kisses desperately, as a plant needed water. The last few moments had told her that. She felt as if she would die without them.

Brett's breathing roughened. 'Don't you? Then you're bloody good at simulation.'

Claire's heart beat violently inside her ribcage and her fingers twitched to slap Brett's face, as if hitting him would get rid of the pent-up guilt and pain and rage inside her.

Brett took a deep breath then raked his fingers through his hair in an impatient gesture. 'Look, I told you. It shouldn't have happened. It was just one of those things. At the time it felt—right.' He shook his head impatiently. 'This probably sounds crazy, but for a moment there I thought... Oh, I don't know what I thought. Forget it. Maybe we've met in a previous life. Reincarnation! Isn't that how some people explain *déjà vu*? Perhaps we were once lovers.'

Claire stared at him aghast. 'That isn't funny,' she said in a small, tight voice.

'No, it isn't, is it?' Brett agreed and walked out of the room and slammed the door.

CHAPTER FIVE

'YOU slut! You dirty little slut! I knew something like this would happen.' Claire's mother's voice was shrill with outrage and disgust.

Claire tossed fretfully in her sleep and clammy perspiration soaked her body as vividly confused memories invaded her dreams.

Skilful, male hands caressed her and lean hips moved in slow, sensuous circles against her thighs. She arched in restless frustration, seeking relief for the sweet, aching need building inside her.

'Spend the rest of your stay in Sydney with me,' Brett's voice urged her.

It was what she had longed to hear. A feverish desire to agree overwhelmed her. 'Yes... Oh, yes!'

'I've got to go away on business for a couple of days, but when I get back we'll spend the rest of the time together.'

A yellow sunburst flooded her mind before black-rimmed clouds edged its dazzling beauty.

A routine telephone call home and then the shock of hearing her father's words. 'Your mother's ill, maybe dying. And it's all your fault. Get a flight home straight away.'

Desperation and guilt raked her insides ragged. Somehow she must let Brett know what had happened.

Frantically she scribbled a note. 'Darling Brett, please contact me in England.'

Claire woke suddenly to find herself icy cold, her duvet in a heap at the side of the bed, her whole body in the grip of a terrible spasm of trembling.

It was the same dream—or perhaps nightmare was the better word—that she'd had for months after her return to England, and what shocked her most was the intensity of the sensations it aroused. It left her body feeling like a wound-up spring, stretched to an unbearable pitch of alternating desire and despair.

Her ghostly reflection stared back at her from the mirror. Her pale skin was covered with tiny goose-bumps, but her face was flushed and her breasts, made fuller and rounder by child-bearing, felt taut and heavy, their rosy pink nipples standing proud and erect.

There was no mistaking their state of sexual arousal and a wave of shame swept over Claire as she realised just how vivid her dream had been. In it she had imagined Brett making love to her and now her inflamed body was fretfully unfulfilled.

Slipping on her robe, she went to check on Emily. Evidently her mother's fevered tossing and turning had not disturbed her; she was sleeping peacefully, one fist curled delicately against her cheek.

How she envied her daughter's peaceful contentment, so at variance with her own charged state. Getting back into bed, Claire huddled beneath the duvet. It was only five o'clock in the morning, but she knew she would not easily get to sleep again. Involuntarily her thoughts went to Brett, asleep at the other end of the house. She imagined his lean, hard body naked beneath the bed cover-

ings, and a violent urge to go to him almost overwhelmed her.

Stop it! she raged against the savage longing. Have
you no shame? Memories of the pain Brett had inflicted
on her were as powerful as if the wounds were freshly
made.

She closed her eyes tightly, but inevitably her thoughts
drifted back to those early days after her return from
Sydney.

How often had she wondered what might have been
if she had not immediately complied with her father's
harsh demand that she should return to England but had
instead waited for Brett's return to Sydney. Would things
have turned out differently or would it simply have post-
poned the inevitable?

Perhaps if she had been able to speak to Brett and
explain what had happened, at least on the telephone . . .
But she hadn't known where he was or how to contact
him. Belatedly she had realised how woefully ignorant
she was of all the practical details of his life: where he
worked, friends; even his telephone number was ex-
directory.

In the brief week they'd spent together those practi-
calities hadn't seemed important. Their apartments were
situated so close together in the complex that communication hadn't been a problem.

Thus she'd had to resort to a frantically scribbled note,
explaining what had happened and giving Brett her
parents' address and telephone number in England and
asking him to contact her as soon as possible. She'd
posted the letter in his mail slot so he would receive it
as soon as he returned, albeit after she'd left.

The journey back to England had been a nightmare. Her mind had swung from one state of despair to another. Would he understand the note? Would he be able to read her writing? Would he contact her? A multiple pile-up of questions had crashed into each other, creating chaos inside her head.

And on top of all that had been the heavy burden of guilt she'd felt for what had happened to her mother. Her father had made it quite clear that he held her 'ridiculous jaunt' to Australia responsible, and perhaps he was right. How will I ever forgive myself if anything should happen? she had asked herself over and over again.

Once back in England, though, she had learned that her mother's condition was not as serious as her father had led her to believe. Angina was diagnosed rather than a heart attack, and there was no question of it being life-threatening.

It was the bleakest Christmas that Claire had ever known; in between daily visits to the hospital and helping her father in the shop she had nearly worn her nerves to shreds waiting anxiously for the postman's visits and trembling every time the telephone rang.

After Christmas she had contacted Duncan and told him apologetically that she couldn't return to work. Her mother had needed rest and care and her father couldn't run the shop alone. The only option had seemed for her to stay with them at least for a while.

Duncan had been wonderfully understanding and had told her to get in touch if she ever needed a job.

As December had given way to January, her mother's health had improved daily, but Claire had got paler and weaker. She had gradually realised that she could no longer put the changes taking place in her body down to the change of climate and stress. When she missed her second period she had knew for certain she was pregnant.

The discovery had come as a terrible shock, but still she had clung to the desperate hope that it was something she and Brett would face together.

Although she hadn't had any word from him, she had convinced herself it was only a matter of time. She had lost count of the excuses she had made for his continuing silence: her note hadn't reached him; he had lost her address; his letters had got lost in the post.

So she had continued to write, not just once, but ten times in total, until even she'd been unable to come up with any more excuses. She'd had to face the fact that Brett hadn't contacted her because he didn't want to. It was as simple and as devastating as that.

By February, she'd known she had to break the news of her pregnancy to her parents. Their reaction had been predictable. Her mother had been loudly disgusted and outraged and her father had been full of silent reproach and condemnation.

'And what are you going to do about it?' her mother had demanded.

'I don't know,' Claire had admitted honestly. Desperately hoping to hear from Brett, she had put off any thoughts about the future.

'Well, you'd better make your mind up quickly. I understand abortions are very difficult to arrange if you leave it too long.'

Every drop of colour had drained from Claire's face at hearing her mother's words. 'An abortion! Who said anything about an abortion?'

'You surely don't intend to keep it.'

'My baby's not an *it*,' Claire had protested in horror. 'It's your grandson or granddaughter.'

Her mother's cold, thin features had been like chiselled ice. 'If you'd gone through the proper channels, perhaps. If you'd met a decent man and got married. But you can hardly expect us to welcome the product of some sordid little affair as our grandchild.'

'It wasn't sordid. I love him,' Claire had sobbed.

'Love him! You stupid girl! You don't know the meaning of the word. What you felt was lust. He used you, that's all.'

Distraught, Claire had retorted, 'And if I don't know the meaning of the word, whose fault is it? What Brett and I had was the closest thing to love I've ever known. And he didn't use me. I wanted him every bit as much as he wanted me.'

Her mother had struck her then, leaving a bright red weal across one cheek. 'Good God! Have you no shame? How dare you say such things to me? Did we bring you up to hold decent Christian values in such low esteem?'

'And what's decent and Christian about aborting an innocent baby?' Claire had demanded, clutching her cheek and racing from the room.

Two days later, her parents had issued their ultimatum. They were not prepared to accept an illegitimate grandchild in their lives. Either Claire had an abortion or they wanted no further contact with her.

The ultimatum had left her with no choice as far as Claire was concerned. No matter what, she couldn't have considered aborting her child.

In desperation, she had telephoned Helen and told her what had happened. Helen had been wonderful. Without any kind of drama, she had immediately invited Claire to stay with her as long as necessary.

Claire hadn't seen her parents since. She had written to let them know where she was, first at Helen's, then the hostel, then Sandwood, and to tell them that they had a granddaughter called Emily. But she'd never received any reply.

Eventually Claire must have dozed off into a restless sleep and she woke suddenly to the sound of the telephone ringing.

Sleepily pulling on her dressing-gown, she ran downstairs to answer it. It was Elspeth.

'Hello, Claire; sorry, did I wake you? I know it's early, but I'm going to be tied up in meetings all day and I did want to give you a bit of warning.'

Claire frowned. 'Warning of what?'

Elspeth continued. 'For once, the kids are all away this Easter and Duncan and I thought it would be fun to come up to Sandwood for the long weekend. We'll be setting off this afternoon so we should be with you around eight o'clock tonight.'

'That...that'll be lovely,' Claire stammered, uncertain how she would cope with an influx of visitors. And also wondering how much of the tension they, particularly Elspeth, would pick up on.

'We're dying to see you and Emily, and Brett of course. How's he been, by the way?'

'He—er—he seems well,' Claire muttered, not liking to admit that they'd hardly spoken to each other for two days.

'He's not giving you a hard time, is he?' Elspeth demanded, obviously picking up a discordant note in Claire's voice.

'No,' Claire lied.

'Hmm.' Elspeth didn't sound entirely convinced. 'Well, you can give him some news to cheer him up. Tell him we're bringing Sandy with us.'

'Sandy?'

'Hasn't he mentioned her? Sandy's his fiancée.'

Claire's hand shook so violently that she nearly dropped the receiver. Fiancée! Brett was engaged to be married! Icy cold fingers tightened round her heart, making it miss a beat.

'Are you all right? You've gone very quiet,' Elspeth asked with concern.

Claire tried to swallow. Her mouth suddenly felt very dry. 'Yes . . . yes. Sorry.'

'That's OK; I just wanted to ask if you wouldn't mind airing our bedroom. It hasn't been used for a while so I expect it's a bit damp. Sandy will probably just go in with Brett so don't worry about making up one of the spare rooms.'

Claire felt horribly giddy, as if she was about to faint. As the housekeeper there were probably all sorts of questions she should be asking, about food likes and dislikes and that kind of thing, but her throat muscles seemed to have gone into convulsions. She was too appalled by what she'd just learned to say anything.

Afterwards, white with shock, she sat at the kitchen table and let her head sink into her hands. Just one shattering blow after another; that was all this last week had consisted of. It was like living in an earthquake zone and never knowing when the next one was going to strike.

Brett had a fiancée. That thought spun round and round inside her head until she felt dizzy. When had they got engaged? she wondered. Had they been together when she'd met him in Australia? He'd never actually denied that there was another woman, had he?

A pain so fierce that she thought there might actually be something wrong with her gnawed at her insides. Was there any treatment for acute misery?

Claire didn't even see Brett until mid-morning when she almost bumped into him in the porch. She'd been outside stacking up the log basket and Brett was just coming out of the door as she went back in. In dark blue jeans and a black polo-neck sweater he was lethally attractive.

'Here, I'll take that,' he offered, seeing her clumsily carrying the heavy basket.

'No!' She backed away from him.

The shocking impact of the morning's phone call hit her again, transforming cheeks already pinked by exertion to a deep shade of scarlet. A hot, angry flush swept right through her body. Right at that moment she hated Brett Jarrett, hated him for making her feel like this, for having the power to hurt her as he had.

Her body stiffened in a rigid posture of defiance. 'No, it's perfectly all right. I can manage,' she informed him coldly.

Black brows jerked together, immediately picking up on her antagonism. 'OK! What's the matter now? Why the cold freeze?' he demanded.

Claire was sick of subterfuge. She didn't see why she should lie about this as well. 'Elspeth telephoned me this morning to tell me she and Duncan are coming up for the weekend. She asked me to give you the good news. They're bringing your fiancée with them.'

An odd expression flitted over Brett's face. 'Sandy?'

'That's her, I would imagine, unless there's more than one,' she said tautly.

'Don't be bloody ridiculous.'

'It's not me who's being ridiculous, it's you,' Claire spluttered furiously. 'You seemed to be having some difficulty matching your fiancée up to the correct name.'

'Will you stop calling her my fiancée?'

'Why? Isn't that what she is?'

'No... Yes,' Brett amended. 'But what's this got to do with you? You're obviously in one hell of a mood.'

If her hands hadn't been totally occupied with holding up the log basket, Claire knew she would have hit him. 'I don't like discovering that I've been kissed by a man who's engaged to marry another woman.'

Brett's eyes narrowed. 'So that's what all this is about.'

This and so much more, Claire thought on a wave of pain so fierce it made her grit her teeth in resistance. 'I don't expect you to understand,' she said tautly. 'Perhaps you think it's all right to go around kissing other women when you're engaged, but I don't.'

'I don't as it happens.' Brett took the wind out of her sails with the agreement.

'But you swallow your scruples and do it all the same,' Claire bit back angrily.

The sharp angles of Brett's face hardened and he took a step towards her. 'Now just a minute. I never planned to kiss you. It just happened.'

And had their relationship in Australia just happened? Was that how he justified everything? 'What a convenient excuse,' Claire snapped. 'I suppose you could say that about everything that happens in your life..."It just happened",' she mimicked mockingly, her dander well and truly up by now.

Brett looked furious. 'Why are you so bloody outraged? Isn't it Sandy who should be having hysterics? It's her that I'm engaged to, not you.'

That thrust found its mark with deadly accuracy. 'I don't like being the other woman,' Claire said coldly, trying to cover her hurt.

'You're not the other woman,' Brett told her cruelly. 'You're exaggerating. It was only a kiss, for God's sake, not a full-blown affair.'

'And you wouldn't have allowed that to "just happen" as well?'

'Would you?' Brett turned the question.

Claire flinched as if he'd hit her. 'No!' she said starkly, wincing at the irony of knowing she already had.

'Well, then, we don't have to worry about my moral scruples disintegrating when yours are so firmly intact, do we?' Brett demanded sarcastically.

'Just keep your hands off me in future.'

'Don't worry, I will,' Brett assured her with tight-lipped fury.

Then he moved forward and swung the log basket up into the air and carried it back into the house ahead of her.

For the rest of the day Claire never stopped. In between looking after Emily, she attacked the housework with a fierce kind of rage.

Her anger was only a veneer, she knew that. Inside she felt as if she were dying. Her throat felt raw and her eyes were unnaturally bright with unshed tears.

She didn't see Brett again and she was deeply thankful she didn't have to face him. By seven o'clock Emily had had her bath and was in her cot asleep, the house was sparkling, and a rich, meaty casserole simmered on the Rayburn while a vegetable quiche cooked in the oven.

As soon as Elspeth and Duncan arrived, she intended to take herself off to bed. She knew she couldn't bear to watch Brett and his fiancée together. Just anticipating it filled her with a kind of sick dread. And she veered away from the thought of them sharing the same bed in horror.

Just after nine o'clock, a car drew up outside. Claire heard voices, then car doors slamming shut, and finally the front door opening. She steeled herself to go through to the hallway to greet the arrivals. There was no curiosity inside her to meet Brett's fiancée. It was bad enough simply knowing she existed without having to put a face to the name.

Elspeth was the first through the door. She came and kissed Claire warmly on the cheek. A tall, slim brunette, in her mid-forties, she was a very attractive woman.

'Hello, my dear. How are you? And where's Emily? I can't wait to see her. She must have grown a lot in the last couple of months.'

'She's—er—she's asleep,' Claire said, too tense to make a more fulsome response. Her mind was completely on edge. She felt as if the slightest push would send her tumbling over the side.

Reluctantly she strained to see past Elspeth into the darkness beyond. Brett had gone outside to help bring in the luggage and he reappeared in the doorway, preceded by someone who looked oddly familiar.

Claire stared at the woman who had just entered, not quite sure if her eyes were deceiving her. When she'd last seen her—if it was the same person—she had been wearing a smart, sarong-style dress and her hair had been longer. Tonight she looked very different in a warm cashmere jacket, chestnut hair cut fashionably short.

But when the woman moved into the light Claire knew it was the same person—Alexandra Carew, Brett's personal assistant in Sydney. They'd met briefly at Brett's apartment when Alexandra had been dropping off some letters for him to sign. Alexandra... Sandy. Her startled mind made the connection. This was Brett's fiancée!

Elspeth performed introductions and Alexandra shook Claire's hand perfunctorily, her attention wholly focused on Brett.

'Did you really need so much luggage for a weekend visit?' he was asking drily.

'Of course, darling. You can never be sure what the weather is going to do in England at this time of year and a girl's got to be prepared for anything. Isn't that right, Elspeth?'

With a faint lift of her brows, Elspeth agreed. 'Of course. Though I have to say I prefer to travel light myself.'

Claire was standing awkwardly under the curve of the stairwell, cast in its shadow, and it was obvious that Alexandra either hadn't seen her properly or had no recollection of having met her before.

Panic flooded Claire's mind in waves. If Alexandra suddenly recognised her now and said something to alert the others, everything would have to come out.

She muttered something about going to check on the dinner and scuttled down the hallway to the kitchen. Once there she sat down in one of the chairs, heart beating wildly, trying to gather her fractured thoughts together.

When had Alexandra and Brett become engaged? Surely it couldn't have been when she was in Sydney. Alexandra had seen her at Brett's apartment. Perhaps Alexandra had been a little cool towards her, but she certainly hadn't behaved like a jealous fiancée.

And Brett had introduced them quite openly; he had definitely described Alexandra as his personal assistant, with no hint of any deeper relationship between them.

Their engagement *must* have occurred afterwards, then. But when? Before his accident or after? Did it really matter? she demanded of herself.

The fact was that they *were* engaged and, however much her stomach might feel as if it had suddenly been filled with gravel, that was the reality of the situation. However dreadful she might find it, she couldn't pretend it wasn't real.

What she had to worry about right now was what to do about Alexandra. She couldn't rely on Alexandra's simply not recognising her. Brett might have lost his memory, but his fiancée—how she hated that word—hadn't. They were going to spend the whole of the Easter weekend in the same house and Alexandra was bound to recognise her sooner or later.

Teeth biting painfully into her lower lip, Claire tried to reach a decision. Fraught with worry, she realised that she really had no option but to see Alexandra alone. She needn't tell her that Brett was Emily's father. She could simply say that, since Brett had obviously no memory of her anyway, she had seen little point in raking up the past and reminding him of a relationship that was long since over.

Surely Alexandra would agree to keep quiet. After all, what did she have to gain by spilling the beans? Brett was her fiancée; surely she wouldn't want to do anything to jeopardise their relationship. And if Claire could keep Emily out of the way, there was no reason for Alexandra to suspect any link between Brett and Emily.

Claire crept to the kitchen door and listened. She could hear Alexandra saying something in the entrance hall.

'I think I'd like to change before dinner, darling. If you could just show me which one is our bedroom, I'll go up and slip into something a little more comfortable.'

'I've made up a bed for you in the room down the passage,' Brett said evenly. 'I haven't been sleeping very well lately and I'll only disturb you if we're together.'

Alexandra didn't sound altogether pleased at the arrangement. 'But, darling, I haven't seen you for ages. I wanted us to be together.' Her voice dropped. 'In fact I really don't mind if we don't get much sleep. I'm sure we can think of something else to pass the time.'

Brett said something low and smooth and she giggled. 'Well, if you insist. I suppose you've got a point.'

Claire winced at hearing the whispered endearments, although the discovery that Brett and Alexandra wouldn't be sleeping together brought an insane wave of relief. Rationally she knew it didn't stop them making love, but quite illogically some of her pain was alleviated at the knowledge that at least they wouldn't be spending the whole night in each other's arms.

The news that Brett hadn't been sleeping well came as a surprise. Hadn't he told her there was no danger of Emily disturbing him as he slept so soundly?

She watched Brett and Alexandra go up the stairs together, their arms entwined, and Brett come down again a few minutes later to join Elspeth and Duncan in the drawing-room.

Now was her chance. If she didn't go now it would be too late. She would have to serve dinner soon and Alexandra was almost certain to recognise her then.

Her feet felt as if they were weighted down with lead as she climbed the stairs and moved along the passageway. A light shone beneath one of the bedroom doors and she guessed that was the room Brett had put Alexandra in. Why hadn't he asked her to get it ready? she wondered. Perhaps he'd wanted to avoid her as much as possible after their confrontation this morning.

Her fingers trembled as she lifted her hand to knock tentatively on the door.

'Come in,' Alexandra called.

Barely able to move for the shaking of her entire body, Claire entered the bedroom.

Alexandra was standing at the wardrobe, hanging clothes up. She peered round the door as Claire came in, looked at her closely, then frowned.

'Don't I know you from somewhere?' she asked.

Claire nodded. 'We...we met in Sydney.'

Alexandra's grey eyes widened and then narrowed. 'Sydney? At Brett's apartment?'

'That's right.'

Alexandra's features lost all their beauty as they screwed up in fury. 'What the hell are you doing here with Brett?'

Claire fluttered her hands in a desperate bid to get Alexandra to keep her voice down. 'You don't understand...Brett...Brett doesn't remember me.'

'What do you mean, Brett doesn't remember you?' Alexandra screeched, not one bit mollified.

'He doesn't remember me because of his amnesia. He's forgotten me and I...I thought it best to leave it like that. None of the family know anything about Brett and me meeting, you see, and I...I wanted to ask you not to say anything.'

Alexandra swung her hands on to her hips, swathed in a beautifully cut, checked wool skirt. 'Is this some kind of trick?'

'Trick?'

'Yes, all this talk about Brett not knowing who you are. What the hell are you up to?'

'Nothing,' Claire denied desperately.

MILLS & BOON

Discover
FREE BOOKS
AND
FREE GIFTS
From Mills & Boon

As a special introduction to
Mills & Boon Romances we will send you:

16 FREE Mills & Boon Romances
plus a **FREE TEDDY** and **MYSTERY GIFT** when you
return this card.

But first - just for fun - see if you can find and circle four
hidden words in the puzzle.

R	D	A	V	R	Y	B	X	N	M
B	O	O	K	N	C	A	S	P	Y
Z	G	M	N	B	U	L	T	R	S
R	T	N	A	N	E	F	T	A	T
D	H	I	A	N	V	K	D	M	E
N	W	L	K	H	C	O	W	S	R
O	C	O	M	U	T	E	D	D	Y
I	L	V	Z	L	P	B	I	T	E
F	E	E	J	S	G	I	F	T	P
S	P	N	S	E	T	I	N	R	E

**The hidden
words are:**

MYSTERY
ROMANCE
TEDDY
GIFT

Now turn over to claim your
FREE BOOKS AND GIFTS

Free Books Certificate

Yes Please send me FREE and without obligation 16 specially selected Mills & Boon Romances, together with my FREE teddy and mystery gift. Please also reserve a special Reader Service subscription for me. If I decide to subscribe, I shall receive 16 superb Romances every month for just £28.80, postage and packing FREE. If I decide not to subscribe I shall write to you within 10 days. The FREE books and gifts will be mine to keep in any case. I understand that I am under no obligation whatsoever. I may cancel or suspend my subscription at any time simply by writing to you. I am over the age of 18.

11A3R

FREE TEDDY

MYSTERY GIFT

Ms/Mrs/Miss/Mr _____

Address _____

_____

_____ Postcode _____

Signature _____

Mills & Boon
Reader Service
FREEPOST
P.O. Box 236
Croydon
Surrey CR9 9EL

NO
STAMP
NEEDED

Offer expires 30th April 1994. The right is reserved to change the terms of the offer or refuse an application. Offer not valid to current Mills & Boon Romance subscribers. Offer valid only in UK and Eire. Readers overseas please send for details. Southern Africa write to IBS, Private Bag X3010, Randburg 2125, South Africa. You may be mailed with offers from other reputable companies as a result of this application. If you would prefer not to share in this opportunity please tick box ☐

'You really expect me to believe that?' Alexandra demanded sarcastically. 'That you just happening to turn up here is all just some odd coincidence?'

'Look,' Claire beseeched her, 'I know how strange this must all look.'

'Very strange,' Alexandra sneered.

'But it really is all just a coincidence. I used to work for Duncan before I went to Australia. When I met Brett I never even knew he was Duncan's brother... You've got to believe me. I didn't even know there was any connection between the two of them until a week ago when Brett arrived here.'

'And just what were you doing here anyway?'

'I look after the house for Duncan and Elspeth. I'm their housekeeper.'

'It's not much of a job,' Alexandra said derisively.

It is when you're out of work, homeless, and have a baby to support, Claire wanted to scream. 'No,' she agreed quietly, 'it isn't. But it suits me. You see since... since we met my circumstances have changed a little.'

'Really? How?' Alexandra asked icily.

Claire's nails dug painfully into her palms. 'I...I have a baby. The... the father and I split up. Emily and I are on our own.'

'I know.'

'You know? How?'

Alexandra shrugged. 'Elspeth must have mentioned it... or Duncan. Does it matter?' she demanded impatiently.

'No! I just didn't realise you knew.'

'Oh, I know all right,' Alexandra said nastily. 'At least I knew that the housekeeper, or whatever you call yourself, had a kid. What I didn't know was that it was *you*.'

She said the word with such venom that Claire almost recoiled. 'It needn't make any difference,' she said desperately.

'Needn't make any difference? How can it not make a difference?' Her eyes narrowed spitefully. 'You had a relationship with *my* fiancé.'

'It . . . it was a long time ago,' Claire stammered. 'And very brief.'

'Yes,' Alexandra agreed harshly. Suddenly she looked uncomfortable. Her fingers played with string of pearls at her throat. 'And you say Brett doesn't remember you? Not at all?'

Claire felt tears sting the backs of her eyelids and furiously blinked them away. 'That's the point. When I . . . I realised Brett didn't remember ever meeting me, I decided not to say anything. I saw no point in raking up events from the past for no reason. I haven't said anything to Brett or Elspeth or Duncan and I . . . I wanted to ask you to do the same. Please! This job means a lot to me. I can't risk losing it. Emily and I would be homeless. I have nowhere else to go.'

Alexandra swung away and spoke with her back to Claire. 'And all you want is for me to say nothing. To pretend I've never met you before in my life?'

'I'm sorry,' Claire apologised. 'I know it's deceitful, but I really feel that would be best for everyone.'

There was a long pause and then Alexandra said, 'Yes, I think perhaps you're right.'

'You'll agree, then ... to keep silent.'

Alexandra turned back, her expression glacial. 'As far as I'm concerned I've never met you before in my life. You're nothing but a stranger.'

CHAPTER SIX

ELSPETH came into the kitchen just as Claire was preparing to serve up the dinner. There was the casserole and a cheese and broccoli quiche, new potatoes and honey-glazed carrots, and an apple crumble was browning in the oven for dessert.

'Mmm, smells delicious.' Elspeth sniffed appreciatively. 'I'm ready for this. The motorway was dreadful. Traffic jams almost all the way. We could only stop for a quick cup of coffee otherwise we wouldn't have got here till after midnight.'

'Oh, dear! You must have had a terrible journey,' Claire murmured, trying to concentrate. Oh, God! She'd just nearly dropped the casserole, her hands were shaking so much.

'Can I help?' Elspeth offered.

'You could take the plates through to the dining-room. They're warming in the top oven,' Claire said gratefully.

Elspeth grabbed a pair of oven gloves and opened the oven door. 'We need another one. There's only four here,' she said.

Claire frowned. 'Is someone else coming for dinner?'

Elspeth laughed. 'For you, silly.'

'No, I couldn't,' Claire protested, horrified. 'It's family, and besides, I promised myself an early night.'

Elspeth glanced at her watch and said firmly, 'It's only nine-thirty. You can't possibly go to bed yet. Besides, we regard you as part of the family too. Duncan and I will be very hurt if you don't join us.'

And Brett and Alexandra will be absolutely furious if I do, Claire thought despondently. Alexandra might have agreed to keep quiet about their meeting in Australia, but Claire had no wish to push her theatrical talents beyond the minimum required. The less she and Alexandra had to see of each other, the less likely were any unpleasant disclosures. She tried again. 'No, really——'

But Elspeth interrupted her. 'To be honest, I'd be glad of the company. No doubt Duncan and Brett and Sandy will start discussing business... Brett's bound to want to catch up on what's happening at the Sydney office... and I've come up here to get away from all that for a few days. You can tell me all about Emily. Is she crawling yet?'

Elspeth's matter-of-fact kindness robbed Claire of any more spur-of-the-moment excuses and reluctantly she found herself getting an extra plate from the cupboard and slipping it on top of the stack already in Elspeth's hands.

Sitting down at dinner with the others was the last thing she wanted. Watching Alexandra and Brett together would be little short of unbearable, and listening to them discussing wedding plans would be sheer torture. She shuddered as a far too vivid picture of them as bride and groom took form in her mind: Brett, tall and dark in an expensively tailored morning suit, and Alexandra, exquisitely fragile in white.

Claire felt sick and utterly and ridiculously betrayed. Hurrying upstairs, she changed quickly out of her jeans

into a demure cotton dress. Its style wasn't particularly
flattering, but then she wasn't wearing it to impress,
merely to try to make herself as inconspicuous as
possible.

Her hands were shaking so much that it was impossible to apply any make-up and even her hair seemed
less biddable than usual. Finally she looked at herself in
the mirror. God! I wish I hadn't agreed to this, she
thought, staring at her pale reflection and running
clammy hands over the gentle curve of her hips.

Once in the dining-room, she fussed unnecessarily with
the cutlery at the table while waiting for the others to
come in. Two knives were crossed and she hastily
straightened them. Weren't crossed knives supposed to
be warning of a quarrel? she thought nervously. No
guesses who would be quarrelling; Alexandra was certain
to be furious at finding her here and she guessed Brett
would be none too pleased either.

Duncan sat at the head of the table, with Alexandra
and Elspeth on either side of him, leaving Claire to sit
opposite Brett. His dark presence across the rich, polished surface of the mahogany table was quite un-
nerving and her stomach felt so knotted that she was
sure she wouldn't be able to eat a thing.

He'd changed into a navy silk shirt and dark trousers
which made him look leaner and more powerful than
ever. If he was surprised to find her there, he concealed
it well. Only a slight narrowing of his eyes as they fell
on her betrayed any reaction whatsoever.

Alexandra however registered her inclusion with barely
disguised hostility. 'I didn't know you'd be eating with
us...Clara, isn't it?' she said tautly.

'Claire,' Elspeth corrected her smoothly. 'And of course Claire will be joining us for meals. She's just like one of the family.'

'You and Duncan have a wonderfully progressive attitude towards your employees,' Alexandra murmured coolly.

Elspeth gave her a small smile. 'I hope *you've* always found that to be the case,' she said pointedly, reminding her that she too was an employee of Atlas Engineering.

'Oh, I have,' Alexandra agreed, picking up on the subtle put-down. She wound her arm possessively through Brett's and gazed at him with huge grey eyes. 'I haven't any complaints about *my* employer, none at all. I'm sure I won't have any when he's my husband either. Which reminds me, we really must get round to setting a date for the wedding, darling.'

Nausea churned in Claire's stomach and she wondered if she was going to be sick.

Brett's hard-edged mouth curved briefly as he gently disengaged her arm. 'I think you'll find you need both hands for eating, Sandy.'

Evidently irritated at Brett's ignoring her attempt to introduce the subject of weddings, Alexandra pouted and for some reason flashed Claire an angry look, as if it were her fault.

Oblivious to such undercurrents, Duncan forked a hearty portion of casserole into his mouth. 'Mmm, this is good. All this nouvelle cuisine is all very well, but you can't beat home-cooking, I always think. It's excellent, my dear.' He smiled at Claire.

Claire tried to smile back, but her jaw muscles ached with tension. She couldn't possibly chew anything and was simply manoeuvring her small helping from one side of the plate to the other.

'It's hardly a good recommendation when the cook seems disinclined to eat her own offerings,' Alexandra said acidly, watching Claire's efforts at rearrangement.

'I'm not very hungry,' Claire murmured.

'Yet you look as if you've got a good appetite normally,' Alexandra said, pointedly eyeing Claire's curvaceous breasts and hips. She was so slim that she looked as if she must be on a permanent diet.

'Yes, hasn't Claire got a lovely figure?' Elspeth said, deliberately pretending that Alexandra's remark had been a compliment.

'You like your women skinny, don't you, darling?' Alexandra smiled winningly at Brett. 'Of course, it hardly matters here where everyone has to wear so many clothes to keep warm anyway, but back in Australia the slightest excess flab shows up in a bikini.'

'Talking about Australia, when are you going back?' Brett demanded, his blue eyes suddenly very cool.

For a moment Alexandra looked piqued. 'Don't you mean *we*, darling? I rather hoped you'd be coming back with me.'

'I can't. Not yet,' Brett said tersely.

'Why not? You're fully recovered now. The doctors said——'

'I know what the doctors said.'

'Well, then?'

Brett's eyes glittered with annoyance. 'I'll return when I'm ready. But that's no reason for you to stay on in England any longer than is necessary.'

Alexandra's top lip quivered. 'You make me sound superfluous.'

'Don't be ridiculous,' Brett said impatiently. 'Dan Arnold has been holding things together pretty well, but I'm sure he could do with some help. You're needed there,' he added, softening the blow.

Alexandra looked only slightly mollified. 'Well, if you really think that's where I could be most useful.'

'I do,' Brett insisted, then, more gently, 'It'll only be for a short time. I'll be back in Sydney as soon as I can.'

To Claire, who had watched the exchange through eyes made larger and deeper by the pallor of her skin, those last words brought a fresh wave of misery. How soon? she wondered.

God knew, she should have wanted Brett gone from here as soon as possible, but the thought of his returning to Sydney—and Sandy—churned her insides like a whisk.

As if realising that their last bickering exchange had hardly cast herself and Brett as a doting couple, Alexandra set out to redress the balance. Stretching her hand across the table towards Claire, she said, 'Have you seen my engagement ring? Isn't it beautiful?'

The ring, a brilliant ruby surrounded by diamonds, was indeed beautiful. 'Yes...it...it's lovely,' Claire agreed, trying to issue the words from a throat as dry as parchment.

'When we bought it, Brett said the ruby reminded him of the colour of my hair, didn't you, darling?'

'If you say so,' Brett agreed tautly.

Alexandra gave a self-conscious little laugh. 'I'm sorry, sweetheart. Of course, you don't remember, do you?'

'No.'

Claire's frowning look flitted from one to the other of them.

'Brett doesn't actually remember us getting engaged,' Alexandra informed her with a cool smile. 'It was all very sudden. Brett asked me to marry him only days before the accident. When he came round he didn't remember a thing about it. I was a bit upset about him forgetting, but the doctors assured us it was perfectly normal. Even the most momentous events can be wiped out by amnesia, they said. Isn't that right, darling?'

'Apparently so,' Brett drawled, sounding bored.

Despite the appalling pain such details inflicted on her, Claire couldn't help wondering why Alexandra had been tactless enough to bring all of them up in front of Brett. He felt the burden of his memory loss badly enough as it was. Why remind him unnecessarily?

Surely as his fiancée she should be trying to offer him comfort, not compounding his sense of frustration. Was she so determined to make Claire suffer that she didn't care about making Brett suffer in the process?

'I'll go and get the pudding,' she offered in an attempt to change the subject, and got up from the table quickly.

The apple crumble was cooked to perfection, its top a lovely, toasty brown. Claire eased it out of the oven and then nearly dropped it as Brett came into the kitchen carrying a stack of dirty plates.

God! He was gorgeous. He was like a lean, fine-boned racehorse. A wave of longing swept over her and hot crimson flooded her cheeks as she acknowledged the wrongness of such yearnings.

Disconcertingly he set the plates down and then edged a hip on to a corner of the table only inches away from her.

'Was there something you wanted?' she asked stiffly.

'I wanted to explain . . . about Sandy.'

'There's nothing to explain,' Claire said tautly, moving away, and then gave a small gasp as Brett's fingers curved round her arm, holding her back.

'I think there is. You were right this morning when you said I should have told you about her. You had every right to be angry.'

Brett hadn't let go of her and his encircling fingers were doing strange things to her bloodflow. Rather than constricting it, they seemed to be making it pump more feverishly than ever.

'All right. Now would you mind letting go of me?' she requested, trying to sound cool despite the electrifying effect of his hold upon her.

Abruptly his grip tightened. 'Dammit! Is that all you can say?'

'What else do you want me to say?' Claire demanded. 'I accept your apology, but that doesn't mean I approve of what you did. You had no right to kiss me. No right at all.'

'Don't sound so bloody censorious about it. You don't know anything about Sandy and me——'

'I know that you're engaged,' Claire interjected curtly.

His eyes darkened at that. 'Why the hell do you have to keep reminding me of that? Do you think I'm unaware of it?'

'You didn't seem in any hurry to remember it yesterday.'

Brett's eyes made a rapid, thorough search of her face. 'Yesterday...' He paused, his gaze lingering with obvious reluctance on her mouth. 'Yesterday I was having difficulty remembering a great many things...like where I might have met you before.'

Fear leapt in Claire's throat. 'I...I told you we haven't met.'

Without warning, Brett's fingers released her arm to move upwards, cupping her jaw. Almost unconsciously he ran a searching thumb along the taut curve. 'Why are you so sure of that?' he demanded softly. 'Or, perhaps, why are you so determined to convince me of it?'

His touch was doing strange things to her, weakening her bones and rendering both anger and fear impotent. She felt herself grow breathless and limpid. 'B-because it's true,' she managed.

'Then why do I get this odd feeling that I am merely rediscovering what was once familiar when I'm with you?'

'I d-don't know.'

Brett frowned. 'Neither do I,' he said slowly. The movement of his fingers stilled as if he had only just realised what they were doing, like some part of him acting independently of his will.

Abruptly he let go of her and raked his fingers impatiently through his hair. 'Have you any idea what it's like waking up from a coma and being informed you're engaged yet having no recollection of ever having proposed?'

Ravaged by an intense despair, Claire shook her head numbly.

'It's difficult for Sandy too,' Brett said harshly. 'It's hardly flattering to discover that your fiancé doesn't have any memory of getting engaged.'

'But...but those memories will come back, given time,' Claire said quietly, issuing the reassurance she knew he needed, yet knowing she wasn't really talking about Alexandra at all, but about the week the two of them had shared. But by then it would be too late. By then Brett would be far away and married to Alexandra.

They were both silent for a moment, each engrossed in their own private miseries, then Brett stood up and said roughly, 'You may be right. I'll just have to wait and see.'

Back in the dining-room, the conversation switched to business and soon Brett and Duncan were absorbed in discussion about possible construction projects in the Middle East, with Alexandra throwing in the occasional comment for good measure.

Elspeth turned to Claire. 'I just popped in to see Emily in her cot while you were in the kitchen. Isn't she gorgeous with all those lovely dark curls?'

'How strange that your daughter should be dark when you're so fair,' Alexandra said, picking up on the exchange and obviously not as interested in the conversation between Brett and Duncan as she professed.

Claire's breath caught in her throat. She dared not risk arousing her suspicions. 'My...my mother's hair was dark,' she said. 'I expect she gets it from her.' It was true enough that Emily's grandmother had been a brunette, but really Claire had no doubt that Emily got her dark colouring from her father.

'How old is she?'

'F-four months.' Claire deliberately subtracted a couple of months.

Elspeth chuckled. 'Really, Claire, when you have four children in five years, as I did, there's some excuse for getting the ages wrong. When you only have the one, there's no excuse whatsoever. Emily's six months now; even I know that.'

There was no malice in the correction, but Elspeth wasn't to know the Pandora's box she had opened with that revelation.

Conscious of Alexandra's eyes narrowing on her, Claire felt her mouth run dry. She choked on a mouthful of apple crumble. Coughing helplessly, tears streaming down her cheeks, she spluttered, 'Excuse me . . . I'll have to go and get a drink of water.'

Once in the kitchen, she wet a tissue under the cold tap and dabbed it on her flaming cheeks.

'Are you all right?' Elspeth asked, coming in a few minutes later.

Claire nodded. 'Silly of me, really. M-my crumble just went down the wrong way.'

'You look very flushed. You're sure you're not coming down with anything?'

Claire shook her head. 'No, I'm fine, honestly.' *Idiot*, she reproved herself moments later. Why hadn't she said she was coming down with flu? Maybe then she could have spent the whole of the weekend in bed and avoided the others completely.

'Well, why don't you get along to bed? Alexandra's already gone up. She seemed a bit put out about something. I don't know what, though I couldn't help noticing that she and Brett were a bit edgy with each other over dinner.' Elspeth shrugged. 'Pre-wedding nerves, probably. Anyway, Brett and Duncan will probably chat for ages yet. Leave the dishes. We can do them in the morning.'

Claire managed a watery smile and nodded. 'All right, I'll just tidy a few things away and then I'll be up.'

She sighed as the door closed. Elspeth was so kindly and matter-of-fact that she hated deceiving her like this. What would Elspeth say if she knew the truth? At the very least, she would be hurt and upset to think that Claire hadn't trusted her enough to confide in her; at worst she would be appalled at her subterfuge.

The next morning was glorious; a bright sun shone in a clear blue sky and only a few cotton-wool clouds dappled the greens and purples of the surrounding fells.

Claire had bought some fish for the evening meal and she spent the morning preparing an elaborate recipe which she'd never tried before simply in order to keep herself occupied.

Her insides felt as knotted as the entrails of the fish she'd just been cleaning. Alexandra had come into the kitchen earlier, refused any breakfast, but had stood with a cup of coffee, staring moodily out of the window. She'd looked exquisite in tartan trousers and a maroon lambs-wool sweater, but very tense, her fingers clasped tightly round her coffee-cup.

Claire had sensed she was waiting for an opportunity for them to be alone and had deliberately kept Elspeth engaged in the most fatuous topics of conversation simply to keep her in the kitchen.

Finally, though, Brett had dragged Alexandra off to admire the views over Derwentwater and Claire had heaved a sigh of relief—relief tinged with a wild surge of jealousy as she spotted them, his arm flung casually round Alexandra's shoulders, through the window.

When Emily woke from her morning nap, Claire sat with her in the bedroom, desperate to avoid the moment when she must introduce her to Alexandra. Every instinct told her that seeing Emily would only confirm Alexandra's suspicions. Other people hadn't spotted the likeness between Emily and Brett because they weren't looking for it. Alexandra was.

Perhaps she'd been wrong not to tell her the whole truth from the beginning. However humiliating it might have been, perhaps she should just have thrown herself on Alexandra's mercy and begged her not to say anything.

Her deception was closing in on her; Alexandra suspected the truth, and Brett seemed to be getting closer and closer to it. How long before the trap slammed shut behind her and there was no escape? Then what? If she had feared that Brett might try to take Emily away from her before, that fear had increased a hundredfold now.

Not only did Brett have money, status and influence, he was also about to gain that most valuable asset in child custody cases—a wife. In the eyes of a court, less interested in personalities than appearances, might not Brett and Alexandra appear infinitely more capable of offering Emily a secure home than she, a poverty-stricken single parent?

Claire buried her head in the palm of one hand in despair, hugging Emily to her with the other. She had never felt more alone or more helpless.

Hungry for her lunch and impatient of her mother's confining hold, Emily began to cry. Claire knew she couldn't sit in the bedroom indefinitely and so with leaden feet she made her way downstairs.

CHAPTER SEVEN

To Claire's dismay, Alexandra was the only one there. She was sitting at the table, perfectly manicured nails drumming a monotonous tattoo on its pine surface. As soon as Claire entered the room, the drumming stopped and her gaze focused ruthlessly on Emily as if she'd never seen a baby before.

Her eyes narrowed to two slits of grey metal, as cold and hard as bullets. 'I knew it! That's Brett's child!' she hissed.

Claire's legs turned to jelly and a terrible sense of doom slid over her. She gripped Emily more tightly than ever.

'Isn't she?' Alexandra demanded furiously.

'Yes,' Claire whispered weakly, instinctively knowing that further lies would be useless.

'You neglected that one little detail in your pathetic appeal last night, didn't you? Not only were you here with *my* fiancé, you were here with *his* child. You deceiving little bitch!'

Claire's whole body shook and her voice was shaky. 'I didn't tell you because I didn't want to cause any further trouble. Brett doesn't know. No one does.'

Not in the least appeased, Alexandra said bitterly, 'She's the reason you sent Brett all those letters, I suppose.'

The blood thundered wildly through Claire's head. 'How ... how do you know about my letters?'

There was a moment's silence while Alexandra struggled to hold on to a composure that had slipped badly during the last few minutes. 'Brett told me about them, of course,' she snapped.

'Brett told you...about my letters?' Claire whispered, turning as white as a sheet. Belatedly she realised how the last few days had rekindled the tiny flicker of hope that perhaps Brett had never received her letters.

Listening to Brett talk, learning of his views on parenthood, remembering the man she had fallen in love with, had all contributed to the impossibility of reconciling his attitudes with those of a man who would deliberately ignore the desperate appeals those letters had contained.

But now Alexandra had shattered even that fragile hope with a vicious hammer blow. The letters had gone straight to Brett's apartment in Sydney. Alexandra could not have known about them unless Brett had told her of them, perhaps even shown them to her. Oh, God! How could he have betrayed her so cruelly?

Alexandra tossed back a sleek curtain of chestnut hair, her composure returning in almost equal measure to Claire's mounting anguish. 'Of course he told me about them. You surely didn't think he'd have kept them secret from me, did you? I'm his fiancée. You were just some cheap tramp he picked up and then discarded.'

Claire flinched as if she'd been hit. *'Some sordid little affair'*! Her mother's sneering description came back to her like a second slap in the face. She'd been horrified by the term, not knowing the real horror was still to come—the horror of realising it was true! Brett had used her in the most callous way a man could use a woman and had then cast her aside like used wrapping paper.

'But you...you and Brett weren't engaged when I met him,' she stammered, trying to block out the greater pain by an almost irrelevant concern with the details of the lesser.

'Not officially, maybe, but we both knew it was only a matter of time.' Alexandra shrugged, 'Oh, I knew he saw other women occasionally, but I didn't interfere. Brett will never be faithful to one woman, I know that. I'm prepared to tolerate the odd affair here and there as long as I know it's me he's coming back to in the end.'

'That's sick,' Claire whispered, appalled at Alexandra's callous description of such a loveless arrangement.

Alexandra's eyes glittered like polished metal. 'How dare you call me sick? Is it any sicker than a woman who tries to trap a man by deliberately getting herself pregnant?'

'I did not deliberately get pregnant...and I didn't try to trap Brett in any way,' Claire protested, adding the subdued denial, 'I didn't even tell him about the pregnancy in my letters.'

'No...' Alexandra conceded unpleasantly. 'But you obviously wanted him to contact you...in Yorkshire, wasn't it?' She threw in another piece of painful evidence to prove her knowledge of Claire's frantically penned pleas. 'Well, whatever you may have hoped and schemed for, your plans have backfired, haven't they? You've ended up a single parent with a kid to support, and Brett's engaged to marry me.'

Tears pressed against the backs of Claire's eyes and she couldn't say anything for trying to swallow the huge lump that had risen in her throat.

'You say you haven't told Brett about *her*?' Alexandra eyed Emily distastefully.

Claire shook her head.

'Well, don't get any ideas about belated confessions, will you?' Alexandra warned fiercely. 'I intend to make sure Brett leaves here with *me* after the weekend, and if he gets any crazy notions about parental responsibilities he may just decide to take *her* with us. Remember that.'

Claire's head jerked upwards as the cruel warning penetrated her terrified thoughts, echoing her own worst fears. Was Alexandra really threatening to aid Brett to take Emily from her if the truth should emerge?

Alexandra hated the sight of Emily, Claire knew that, but she was jealous and furious and bitter enough to do it to hurt her. Claire felt like a condemned prisoner waiting for the axe to fall upon her neck.

She wanted to protest, argue, beg, whatever it took to persuade Alexandra not even to consider such a thing, but her throat was so constricted with fear that she couldn't force a single word out.

Then the moment for appeal was gone as Emily, distressed by the raised voices and charged atmosphere, started to cry. A wave of remorse swept over Claire and she gripped Emily tightly. How could she have subjected her daughter to such an ugly scene?

Moments later, alerted by Emily's crying, Elspeth bustled into the kitchen, fussing over the baby.

'I'm just going to get my coat. Brett and I are going for a walk,' Alexandra announced, throwing Claire a look of pure dislike and silent threat as she left the room.

'Shall I give Emily her lunch?' Elspeth offered cheerfully, and Claire silently handed her over. Her nerves were so ravaged that she didn't feel as if she could cope with even the most mundane task at the moment.

'What's the matter?' Elspeth asked, competently settling Emily into her high chair. 'You've gone deathly pale.'

Then, when Claire didn't say anything, 'What on earth's going on, Claire? I know something's wrong. At first I thought Alexandra and Brett were responsible for the strained atmosphere . . . they're obviously not getting on very well . . . but you seem upset as well. Do you all know something I don't?'

Claire struggled to make sense of the tormented chaos inside her head. She felt terrible, as if a giant hammer was knocking the stuffing out of her. 'I . . . I don't think Alexandra likes me,' she managed at last in the face of Elspeth's expectant look. What a ridiculous understatement. Alexandra loathed her.

Elspeth shook her head and frowned. 'But why should she dislike you? She doesn't even know you. I don't understand her at all. She works as Brett's personal assistant, you know, and she's probably very competent at her job, but it never struck me that there was anything but a professional relationship between them. When she showed us her engagement ring after the accident, Duncan and I were rather surprised. Brett never mentioned anything to us about getting married. Of course, at the time, he was so ill that we didn't think much beyond his recovery. Now, though, I can't help wondering if they aren't making a mistake. I didn't think Brett was exactly overjoyed to see her last night, did you?'

Claire managed to make some sound that could have meant anything. Icy fingers were inching their way down her spine as Alexandra's warning thundered through her ears, blocking out everything else.

What if the circumstances of Brett's and Alexandra's engagement *were* a little strange and what if it *wasn't* altogether a success? Why should she care? They richly deserved each other, Brett for being such a bastard and Alexandra for being such a bitch!

One thing she knew: she would never allow them to take Emily from her!

Elspeth spooned a mouthful of puréed stew into Emily's mouth. 'Don't let Alexandra get to you, dear. I imagine she and Brett have had a few terse words and she's taking her anger out on you. It's probably nothing personal. Just ignore it.'

Ignore it! Claire longed to send both Brett and Alexandra into oblivion. She never wanted to see either of them again.

'Hope springs eternal in the human breast'. Pope's words came back to her like a cruel joke. Well, hope didn't spring in her breast any longer. That seed had been smothered beyond revival. All she had now was a cold, hard block of ice where her heart had once been. And every time she thought about Brett discussing her letters with Alexandra it hardened a little more.

Somewhere in the distant recesses of her mind a tiny voice reminded her how at variance that chilling image was with her own judgement of the man, but it was swamped by the tide of pain and bitter sense of betrayal which engulfed her.

Minutes later Duncan walked into the kitchen, followed by Brett. Claire stared at him with cold disdain, drawing a hard, narrowed look in return.

Totally bemused by the presence of so many people, Emily decided she'd had enough to eat and instead started banging her spoon on the plastic feeding tray, then chuckled with delighted satisfaction when she saw she'd got everyone's attention, Brett's included. He slid her an indulgent smile which she immediately returned, fanning her long dark lashes against her cheek with almost flirtatious pleasure.

Then, to Claire's dismay, she discarded her spoon on the floor and immediately raised both arms towards him. Before Claire could even move, Brett had reached down and lifted her up, his long, lean fingers curling round her small body, holding her close.

Claire watched the unconscious display of intimacy between father and daughter with horrified fascination.

As if from a distance, she saw Elspeth give Duncan a surprised look before saying, 'It seems as if you've got a fan there, Brett.'

Quite unselfconsciously, he laughed. 'Females are wonderful at this age. No complaints or recriminations. Just pure, unadulterated adoration.'

Elspeth punched him playfully on the shoulder. 'Chauvinist pig!'

Emily, obviously amused, crowed out loud and Duncan and Elspeth and Brett laughed with her. It was at that moment that Alexandra returned, a navy cashmere jacket slung casually over her shoulders.

She surveyed the little tableau of father and daughter with narrowed eyes, her expression grim.

'What the hell are you doing?' she demanded furiously of Brett.

'What do you mean?' he asked coldly.

'Why are you holding *her* kid?' She jerked her head in Claire's direction, angry grey eyes fixed on Brett.

Claire's legs almost gave way beneath her. She was terrified by the prospect of Alexandra spilling the beans in temper. For a moment her heart seemed to stop beating. '"Her" is Claire and this is Emily. You know their names; why can't you use them? Besides, Emily's not a kid. Kids are the offspring of goats,' Brett said icily.

The skin round his eyes was tight with anger and his mouth was hard. It was obvious to everyone that an even more terse retort was only just kept in check, but Alexandra seemed too incensed to care.

'How would you know?' she screeched. 'You've never been the slightest bit interested in children and now all of a sudden you can't take your eyes off hers.'

'Don't be ridiculous,' Brett said tautly.

'I'm not,' Alexandra retorted wildly. 'You should see yourself. You look positively bloody doting.'

All of a sudden Brett thrust Emily into Elspeth's arms, grabbed Alexandra by the wrist, and yanked her towards the door. 'If you insist on having this conversation, I think it would be better conducted in private,' he said curtly.

Their raised voices could be heard all the way along the corridor.

'What on earth was all that about?' Elspeth said to no one in particular, shaking her head. Then, 'It's all right, darling, no one's cross with you,' as Emily's small mouth puckered.

Instinctively Claire reached across and took her into her arms. Her body was trembling all over as she rocked Emily to and fro, taking almost as much comfort from the small, solid body as her daughter did from her.

'I'm so sorry, Claire; I've no idea why Sandy was in such a foul mood,' Elspeth said apologetically.

'It…it's all right,' Claire said, knowing perfectly well what had triggered Alexandra's furious reaction. She couldn't bear seeing Brett and Emily together.

'Indeed it's not all right,' Elspeth said. 'Sandy may be Brett's fiancée, but that doesn't give her the right to behave like a fishwife, especially not while she's a guest in our home. I intend to have a word with her about it.'

'Oh, please don't,' Claire begged, terrified of making the situation worse.

'Well, I certainly intend to have a word with Brett,' Elspeth said, still ruffled. 'He may be prepared to tolerate those kinds of tantrums, but I'm not. I just hope he knows what he's letting himself in for when he marries her. She's going to be one very demanding wife.'

For the next twenty-four hours, Claire existed in a state of perpetual panic. Fears and anxieties plucked at her nerves like skilled fingers on the strings of a harp, reducing her to almost unintelligible despair as she awaited expected disaster, like an audience anticipating the climax of a Shakespearian tragedy.

She'd seen little of Alexandra and Brett. They had gone out together on the Friday evening and had returned late. Judging by the cool civility they displayed towards each other the next morning, the outing had done little to heal the rift between them.

Vaguely nagging doubts and half-formed questions hovered on the periphery of Claire's mind. An oddly discordant note jangled every time she thought about Brett's and Alexandra's engagement. Why had Brett no recollection of it? Why had Duncan and Elspeth had no inkling of its likelihood? Even her own brief meeting with Alexandra in Sydney had rung no warning bells of any personal intimacy between them.

But Claire savagely shoved such confusions aside. What did they matter? The fact was that Brett and Alexandra *were* engaged. Pondering on the nature of their relationship was futile.

All she could do now was pray that Alexandra would understand it was in nobody's interests to reveal the truth and wouldn't, in a fit of spiteful revenge, disclose all. That dreadful possibility and its consequences were all she cared about.

Once Brett had gone, every hope and dream she had once cherished for their future together would go with him, and she knew that the terrible weight of their loss would be unbearably painful. But until then all her concerns were for her daughter.

While Claire was giving Emily her bath on Saturday evening, Elspeth sought her out. 'It's Duncan's birthday next week,' she said, laughingly splashing water on

Emily's tummy, 'but unfortunately he's going to be abroad, so I've arranged a little get-together tonight instead. Nothing elaborate, just a few friends coming for a drink. Given Brett's and Alexandra's mood, I think anything more might stretch their conviviality to breaking-point,' she added drily.

'What a nice idea,' Claire murmured, thinking that her own desolate mood would not stand too much heartiness either.

'You're invited, of course,' Elspeth said. 'And before you go all coy and say you couldn't possibly join in, Duncan will be very hurt if you don't.'

The excuses which Claire had been busy formulating died on her lips as she recognised that what Elspeth said was true. Duncan had been more than kind to her and it would look very odd if she didn't join the celebrations, at least for a short time. She concentrated on sponging Emily, not wanting Elspeth to see how much the prospect dismayed her.

'Have we any birthday candles?' Elspeth asked. 'I don't think Duncan would quite appreciate the full fifty that the occasion demands, but I've bought a cake, and a few would be nice.'

'I think I've seen some somewhere. I'll search them out,' Claire promised. Then, impulsively giving way to an underlying curiosity, 'Duncan's quite a lot older than Brett, isn't he?'

'Good gracious yes. Brett's only thirty-one. Usually in those cases it's the same father and different mothers. In Duncan's and Brett's case it was reversed. Different fathers, same mother. Apparently she was fond of telling people she'd only made two major mistakes in her life, but as they were made nearly twenty years apart there was some excuse.'

'How horrible!'

Elspeth grimaced. 'Isn't it? She passed on several years ago now and I suppose one shouldn't speak ill of the dead, but to be honest she never was one of my favourite people. She more or less abandoned both the boys when they were very young. I think that's why Duncan was so determined to create a stable home for our children; he wanted them to have what he'd never had. I think Brett'll be the same. He'd never let a child of his go through what he did.'

Elspeth wasn't to know the chill her words sent through Claire. Would Brett consider her able to offer Emily a *stable* home if he found out the truth? Of course he wouldn't! He'd made his views clear enough that day he'd suggested she try to contact Emily's father again. As she was a single parent on the breadline, her provision was woefully inadequate as far as he was concerned.

When Elspeth had gone, Claire slumped at the side of the bath. Two more days! Two more days and then Brett and Alexandra would be gone from her life forever. Surely she could hold out till then?

An hour later, with Emily asleep in her cot, Claire was able to change for the evening. She stared at the contents of her wardrobe, wondering what would be most suitable. Perhaps one of her now discarded maternity dresses would be the most sexless outfit she could choose, but she doubted Alexandra would consider it a tactful choice.

She rifled through her usual uniform of jeans and sweaters. How long was it since she'd worn anything remotely dressy? Not that she wanted to wear something eye-catching, but to deliberately dress down might be construed as being just as attention-seeking as the other.

The silky jade two-piece of tunic top and matching skirt had been a gift from Helen after Emily's birth. Typically Helen had dispensed with the usual gifts of soft toys and baby rattles and had instead bought a practical cot and pushchair for Emily and a highly impractical but rather lovely outfit for Claire.

Claire had never yet had an opportunity to wear it, but it seemed to fit the bill for the evening exactly. The set was casually elegant, but its high-necked top and below-the-knee-length skirt could hardly be regarded as attention-seeking, even by Alexandra's critical eye.

By nine-thirty, there were several small clusters of guests in the drawing-room. In between helping to serve drinks, Claire had spent most of the evening chatting to a James Shepherd, who managed a chain of small art galleries in the Lake District.

She'd taken care to keep well away from Brett and Alexandra, but every so often caught Alexandra's eye across the room and almost froze at the malice she encountered there.

'We've been very busy over the weekend,' James was saying. 'This warm weather's brought the visitors out in droves.'

'I should think it's been good for the tourist industry as a whole,' Claire murmured.

'Of course we like to consider our galleries a cut above the usual tourist trails,' James said rather pompously.

'You must come and see our Keswick premises for yourself... perhaps next week?'

Claire had no idea what sort of response she gave as at that moment her eyes collided with Brett's, absorbing the impact of their hard blue gaze and feeling the almost magnetic pull of his will reaching out to her across the room. It took every ounce of strength she possessed not simply to walk away from James in mid-sentence and move towards Brett. She felt as if she were being hypnotised.

Suddenly, though, the spell was broken as Elspeth materialised at her elbow. 'Claire, dear, would you mind seeing if there are some champagne glasses in that cupboard? I'm going to bring the cake in shortly and we can drink a toast.'

Gathering the torn shreds of her composure, Claire crouched down by the cupboard, pulled the door open, and then almost groaned aloud as a pile of canvases fell from inside it.

Face turning the colour of beetroot, she rushed to push them together, but it was too late; James was already picking some of them up and thumbing through them. 'These are interesting,' he murmured. 'What wonderful colours. They're not English landscapes, though. 'I'd say they were Australian. This is Ayers Rock, isn't it?'

Everything else in the room seemed to blur as Claire focused on the culpable collection of brilliant browns and reds and ochres in his hands. She'd worked on the canvases during the long, wet winter days here at Sandwood and had tucked them away, forgotten, in the cupboard, never dreaming how they might betray her.

'Yes.'

'Who painted them? You?' James sounded surprised.
Claire nodded weakly.

Duncan peered over James's shoulder. 'They're excellent, my dear. I wouldn't mind buying one myself.'

'Please, have a look at them later... Choose any you want... as a birthday present,' Claire urged, crouching down at the cupboard to extract the champagne glasses Elspeth had requested, and desperate simply to hide the paintings away again before Brett should see them.

But Duncan was not to be rushed; he examined two or three more closely. 'Did you do them from memory or while you were over there?'

'Over where?'

The question was as cold and precise as chipped ice and Claire didn't need to look up to know that it had come from Brett.

Shock deprived her of all powers of speech and it was left to Duncan to say cheerfully, 'Australia, of course. Didn't you know Claire spent three months there? You two obviously have more in common than you realise.'

The innocent irony of that statement made Claire want to cringe with raw horror. Far more than Australia... They had a daughter in common!

She didn't need to look at Brett to know that he was staring at her. She felt his eyes boring into her with all the piercing accuracy of a laser beam. For a moment her heart seemed to stop beating. She'd told him she'd never been to Australia. She'd lied and now he knew it!

Like some providential fairy, Elspeth entered the room at that moment, carrying the birthday cake, its tiny candles spluttering incandescently as the lights were switched off and a chorus of 'Happy Birthday' began.

Blessing the interruption, Claire seized her moment and crept quietly out of the room.

In the hallway she caught sight of her startling reflection in the mirror. Everything about her was far too bright: eyes, cheeks, lips. Even her hair seemed to have absorbed the shocking currents of the past minutes, billowing around her head like an electrically charged storm cloud.

Hurrying on, she raced into the kitchen, but even that one-time haven didn't feel safe any more. Knowing she was acting crazily, that there was no escape, Claire slipped the lock on the back door and went outside.

A full, creamy moon shone in a charcoal night sky and the air was heavy with the scent of pink-tipped magnolia blossoms. Somewhere in the distance a lamb baaed for its mother. It's all so beautiful and so peaceful, Claire thought fretfully. Why can't some of it rub off on to my life?

Suddenly the back door was flung open and Brett stood there, his powerful outline silhouetted by the light streaming out from the kitchen behind him.

Despite the concealing shadows, Claire could see the hard-edged set of his mouth and the taut angle of his jaw. In contrast his teeth had an unearthly whiteness about them.

She shivered with the instinctive fear of a prey who knew it was about to be devoured by its fanged predator.

'Why did you tell me you'd never been to Australia?' There were no gentle preliminaries to cushion the impact, just a fierce, merciless assault.

The night was mild, but her whole body felt as if it had just been coated in ice. She shivered, her brain felt numb, and she was hardly able to issue a word through lips frosted together. 'It... it holds bad memories for me. 'I d-don't like to even think about it.'

He was staring at her, his eyes ruthlessly stripping away the protective layers she would desperately have clung to. 'That's no reason to lie about it,' he said, his voice cold and dismissive.

In the darkness, Brett was all blackness and shadows, a panther in its natural habitat, unperturbed by the horrors of the night. While she, his victim, was lost and utterly afraid.

'I... I didn't mean to lie about it,' she said weakly.

One brow tilted in blatant disbelief. 'Didn't you? As I recall I asked you a straightforward question. It required only a single-word answer. Why was the lie easier to utter than the truth?'

Because she hadn't dared risk the truth... still dared not. The consequences were too terrible even to contemplate. Since the truth couldn't be, then bluster had to be her defence. 'I—I don't wish to discuss this. You have no business interrogating me.' Thus saying, she stepped sideways towards the door, intending to go back into the house, but Brett was too quick for her. In an instant he had turned the key in the lock and pocketed it.

'Open that door at once,' she demanded, in a voice whose authority was audibly weakened by the numbing fear of her secret being discovered.

Brett leaned one hand on the stone wall beside her head, effectively cutting off her escape route. 'No,' he refused succinctly. 'Not until you tell me the truth.'

Fear churned in great waves inside Claire's stomach. 'Alexandra's going to come looking for you in a minute,' she blurted out.

'This has nothing to do with Sandy,' Brett said roughly. 'Leave her out of this.'

Of course! Alexandra was his fiancée while she, Claire, was just 'some cheap tramp he picked up and then discarded'. Wasn't that how Alexandra had described her? Briefly pride trampled roughshod over her fear, squashing it underfoot, and giving free rein to a sudden spurt of anger.

'Why? Don't you think she'd approve of our little moonlight tryst?'

'This is not a tryst,' Brett snarled.

'I'm certain that's how she'll view it if she finds us out here.'

'She won't find us. She's drinking champagne, toasting Duncan's birthday.'

'And you think she won't notice you're not?' Claire demanded. Alexandra's watch on Brett's movements was as accurate as radar. She would know he was missing by now. 'Any minute now she'll come looking for you.' Desperation edged the warning as Claire anticipated the furious scene which would follow.

Indifferent to the warning, he settled the full force of his black-fringed gaze upon her. 'Forget Sandy,' he instructed tautly. 'I'll deal with her. This is between you and me. You lied to me and I want to know why.'

Brett was standing so close to her that his breath fanned her cheek, warming the frozen flesh with its wine-scented heat. She could see the arc of his jawline profiled in the moonlight and the masculine curve of his mouth just inches away from hers.

Suddenly her anger mysteriously ebbed away and all she could feel was the deep, unsteady thudding of her heartbeat. In the darkness, a barn owl hooted and Claire almost jumped out of her skin. 'I don't know why I lied,' she said limply, her voice almost as hoarse as the barn owl's.

'I think you do. Now tell me.'

Claire twisted her face sideways, trying to evade the piercing scrutiny of his eyes. 'I told you. It has bad memories for me. I just want to forget about it.'

'Because of Emily's father?'

She nodded, still not looking at him.

'And that's all?'

'Yes.'

His palm cupped her chin, forcing her back to face him. 'I don't believe you.'

'B-but it's true.'

'It may be true.' Brett disarmed her with the terse acknowledgment. 'But it's not the whole reason. There's more to it than that. From the moment we met there's been something strange between us. Something you know that I don't. I believe we've met before. I believe we met in Sydney.'

Claire's breath was coming so quickly that it shuddered in her throat. 'W-we didn't.'

'Didn't we? Then why does some elusive memory of you keep flickering in my mind and then disappear whenever I try to catch it? Why do you have this effect on me?'

'W-what effect?'

'The same effect I have on you. I can feel your body trembling. Don't fight me, Claire. Don't fight yourself.'

The languid assurance of the words washed over her like molten honey, so seductively sweet that her lips parted in soft anticipation of its taste on her tongue.

She didn't know which of them moved first, but suddenly Brett was so close that it seemed that every part of her body was in contact with his. His kiss was fierce and possessive, capturing her mouth with a raw hunger of almost insatiable need. Her fingers caught in the thickness of his hair, striving even now to lessen the distance between them.

She was caught in an electrical storm. Forked lightning scorched her veins, setting her blood on fire until it burned like molten lava. Sweet, lancing sensuality speared her body, making her bones melt with a hunger so intense that it took her breath away.

Her body, her whole being, had been starved of its essential nourishment and now it sought to fill the vacuum. Her mouth opened willingly beneath Brett's questing tongue, accepting his invasion with urgent longing.

Dreams of this moment had been sweet, but reality was sweeter still. Excitement spiralled through her like a hurricane, sweeping aside all reason. Willingly she arched against him, throbbing as Brett's mouth stormed each quivering pulse-point in turn.

His lips sought the blue-veined hollow at the base of her throat while his hand moved to the zip on the back of her tunic top, unpeeling it with almost unbearable leisure. Her breath caught in an agony of anticipation in her throat as she felt his hand slide inside.

Her breasts ached and strained against their lacy covering, swelling with unashamed demands for his touch. Brett did not disappoint them. Skilfully his fingers tugged aside the frail defences to curve possessively round one pouting crest, his thumb grazing the swollen nipple.

Claire gasped as a burst of pleasure exploded inside her, showering trails of incandescent sparks through her body. Her fingers dug deeply into his shoulder, so violent was the shudder which engulfed her, and a muted moan was torn from her throat.

'God! I want you!' Brett said hoarsely. 'Feel what you do to me.' One hand cupped the soft round swell of her buttocks, drawing her against the contrasting hardness of his thighs.

Suddenly the locked door beside them rattled as someone tried to open it. Even as the footsteps receded, Claire froze.

Brett gave a low growl and muttered something unrepeatable.

Heat drained from Claire's body like water from a bath once the plug was pulled. Hazy whorls of passion spiralled briefly and then disappeared. Moments before she had been suffused with fire, now she felt icy cold.

'Get off me,' she whispered fiercely, closing her eyes, as if blocking out the sight of Brett in front of her could in some way lessen the stampeding drive of guilt and rage which forked her body.

Her fingers sought to repair her disarrayed clothing, but were shaking far too much to be more than superficially successful.

Without saying a word, Brett closed his fingers on the recalcitrant zip, drawing it back into place. 'Look at me,' he insisted rawly, his hands closing on her shoulders and forcing her round to face him.

'No,' she denied vehemently, blinking back glittering tears.

'Don't expect another apology,' Brett ground out harshly. 'I have no intention of apologising for what happened. It was inevitable.'

Claire's nails ground painfully into the palms of her hands. 'How dare you——?'

'I dare because it is true,' Brett drawled uncompromisingly. 'Let us be honest about some things at least.'

'Honest!' Claire gritted furiously. 'What's honest about you making love to me? You're engaged to marry Alexandra!'

Even in the darkness of the night, Brett's pupils glowed like two black coals. 'Not any longer,' he said grimly.

CHAPTER EIGHT

MOONBEAMS glanced off Claire's hair, turning it silvery gold in the darkness. 'Pardon?'

'I am not engaged to Alexandra. I doubt I ever was.'

Claire's fuddled brain tried to take in what he was saying, like fighting her way through the shadows which surrounded them. How could he not be engaged to Alexandra? She wore his ring on her finger. He'd placed it there. Her brow pleated. 'I don't understand.'

'You don't have to,' Brett informed her, brushing aside her concern. 'I will speak to Alexandra.'

'But I want to understand,' Claire said fretfully. 'I don't want you to break off your engagement to Alexandra . . . not because of me,' she made the painful addition, knowing it was only half true.

One lean finger grazed the slender length of her throat, setting the pulse there beating rapidly. 'It is impossible to break an engagement that was never made in the first place.' Then, as Claire's frown deepened, 'Trust me. Later I will explain, but first I must talk to Sandy. It would be unfair not to.'

His voice had a rich, mellifluous timbre which washed over her in great, reassuring waves, making her want to melt into it. If only she could trust him. If only she could forget everything and rely on Brett to sort it all out.

But jagged obstacles leapt out of nowhere, forcing her to resist the temptation. Once Brett spoke to Alexandra, she would tell him everything. She would draw every last drop of Claire's blood in revenge for losing him.

'No, please, you mustn't.' Her fingers clutched at his shoulders.

Not ungently, Brett disengaged them. 'Yes, I must,' he contradicted, moving sideways and removing the door key from his pocket.

After the concealing darkness, the light from the kitchen was unnaturally bright. Too bright. Claire felt as if her flushed skin, the dishevelled state of her clothing, the faint gleam of perspiration which damped her brow and slicked her palms, were all illuminated under spotlights.

She went to the sink and filled a glass of water and was just taking a gulp of it when the door was thrust open and Alexandra stood there, her eyes as brittle as broken glass.

'Ah! Here you are.' The words were sharp staccatos. 'At last. I've been looking for you everywhere. Where the hell have you been? I suppose you know all the other guests have gone? Can you imagine what they thought when there was no sign of either of you at the end——?'

'Sandy, you and I have got to talk,' Brett said quietly, interrupting her shrill flow of questions.

'Damn right we've got to talk. About her for one.' Alexandra pointed a long red talon in Claire's direction.

'No, not about Claire, about us,' Brett insisted firmly.

Claire's head felt woolly. She didn't know how much more of this she could take. 'I-I'll leave you alone,' she said, heading towards the door.

'Oh, no, you don't!' Alexandra screeched at her. 'This is all your fault and you're not going to sidle away and pretend it isn't. It's about time Brett knew...'

The blood seemed to be rushing round Claire's head like a washing-machine reaching the end of its cycle. She wondered if she was about to faint. Time seemed to stand still as she waited for Alexandra to utter those fatal words of explanation, but suddenly the spell was broken as Elspeth rushed past Alexandra into the room, her expression grave.

'Claire, you'd better come and have a look at Emily. I heard her crying and popped my head round the door to check on her and she seems very hot.'

Seconds later, Claire was racing up the stairs, guilt raking at her insides as she absorbed the painful fact that while she had been outside with Brett Emily had been ill.

She reached the cot and picked Emily up, horrified to discover that Elspeth was right. Emily felt red-hot and she was crying miserably.

Brett was right behind her and she turned to him now, demanding helplessly, 'Oh, God! What's the matter with her?'

Brett examined her quickly, his touch steady and calm. 'I think it's probably just a high temperature, perhaps in response to some sort of infection. If it is, then it's not serious, but I think we'd better get her to the hospital just in case.'

'Hospital?' Claire almost gagged on the word. It made everything sound so much more serious.

Brett's gaze swept over her face, now almost as pale as Emily's, and he twisted a strand of damp hair behind her ear. 'It's just a precaution, that's all.'

Duncan and Elspeth were hovering anxiously in the doorway. 'I'll call an ambulance,' Elspeth offered straight away, adding apologetically, 'None of us can drive. We haven't had much to drink, but enough to put us over the limit.'

'No, I'll take them,' Brett said immediately. 'I only had a couple of glasses of wine earlier.'

Right at that moment, Claire didn't care who took them as long as they got to the hospital as quickly as possible. 'Let's go now, please,' she pleaded, grabbing a shawl from the cot and wrapping it round Emily's small body.

Downstairs Alexandra met them in the hallway. 'Where are you going?' she demanded of Brett.

'I'm taking Claire and Emily to the hospital,' Brett said tautly.

'But I thought you said you wanted to talk to me,' Alexandra returned petulantly.

Brett's mouth thinned as he made a determined effort to be patient. 'That was before I knew Emily was ill.'

'Can't someone else take them to the hospital?'

'No!'

Alexandra's face set in uncompromising lines. 'Well, if you go now, don't expect to find me here when you get back.'

'All right, I won't,' Brett agreed succinctly and turned to go.

Alexandra's stiff reserve crumpled and she almost threw herself on him. 'Brett, please, don't leave me like this.'

Without particular gentleness, Brett disengaged her arms from round his neck. 'Alexandra, stop it; I must go. The child's ill. If you want to talk to me when I return, then stay. If you don't, then go. The choice is yours.'

Alexandra backed off him then, her stricken features evidence enough of her realisation that she had lost him. Her eyes scanned wildly for some culprit to blame for her loss and fell on Claire. 'You bitch!' she screeched. 'All this is your fault.'

'Shut up, Alexandra,' Brett warned, raw violence in the instruction.

'That's enough, Alexandra,' Elspeth said briskly and urged her into the drawing-room.

A shocked numbness seemed to be working its way through Claire's limbs. She could hardly move. When Brett's arm circled her shoulders to guide her outside, she slumped weakly against him, desperately grateful for the support.

At the hospital, everything, miraculously, was taken out of her hands. On arrival, Emily was immediately whisked into a curtained cubicle to be examined by the duty doctor.

Brett and Claire stood beside her small form stretched out on the white sheeting, watching as the doctor, a woman, shone lights into her eyes and tested reflexes.

Claire was infinitely grateful for the solid wall of Brett's body supporting her from behind, his arm resting possessively on her shoulders.

'What...what do you think, Doctor?' she asked at last as the examination seemed to be coming to an end.

The doctor's smile was reassuring. 'I'm almost certain it's just a viral infection.'

'But she was fine earlier.'

'Babies can develop these rather alarming symptoms very quickly, but it usually looks far worse than it is. The body's natural defence system gets to work very quickly. She'll probably be right as rain by the morning. However, I would like to keep her in for a day or so, just to run some tests and make sure that's all it is.'

'But you are pretty sure it's nothing serious?' Claire asked shakily. 'I mean, she looks so miserable...and she's normally so lively.'

'I'm almost a hundred per cent certain. I doubt very much you've got anything to worry about. Your daughter's going to be fine.'

Her smile took in both Claire and Brett, and Claire immediately realised that the doctor had assumed Brett was Emily's father.

Crazy though it seemed to be denying the truth, Claire felt her cheeks flush with painful colour. 'Oh! But——'

Only Brett's hand tightening on her shoulder silenced her.

'That's good news, thank you,' he said smoothly.

While the doctor instructed one of the nurses on Emily's admission, Claire twisted to face Brett, her heart leaping into her throat as she wondered if he had reached the truth without Alexandra's help. But he merely smiled down at her.

'Relax,' he urged. 'I know she assumed we're both Emily's parents, but why create problems with unnecessary explanations? What does it matter?'

It mattered a great deal because it was the truth, Claire reflected uncomfortably. But the porter arrived then to take Emily to the children's ward and, while Claire was absorbed in that task, Brett's calm suggestion that she should leave the assumption uncorrected seemed to make sense. After all, compared with Emily's well-being, it hardly mattered right now.

For the next few hours, Claire hardly left Emily's side, even sleeping on a small camp bed that the staff set up beside her cot.

By the morning, though, Emily seemed almost fully recovered. A little quieter than usual and a little paler, but, other than that, recognisably normal.

Claire could hardly contain her relief. Despite the reassurances of the casualty doctor, she'd been terrified that there might be some more serious explanation for Emily's condition. Seeing her daughter awake and hungry for her breakfast was wonderfully encouraging.

The paediatric consultant too seemed pleased, concurring with the casualty doctor's diagnosis that Emily had merely got some sort of viral infection, but suggesting they keep her in for another couple of days for tests, just to be absolutely certain.

'But you are sure it's nothing serious?' Claire demanded, hating to think there was even the slightest shred of doubt.

His smile was calm and infinitely soothing. 'Of course I'm sure, Mrs—er...' He consulted his notes.

'Miss... Miss Seymour,' Claire supplied quickly.

To his credit, if he was surprised at all, his expression didn't show it. 'Ah, yes, Miss Seymour. I'm perfectly satisfied from my examination that your daughter's only suffering from a slight ear infection, but I would like the tests done purely as confirmation, nothing more.'

He moved on then to the next patient, a small boy with a broken leg, and Claire was left looking after him, her worries calmed but her composure dented by a quick tug of dismay.

Don't be ridiculous, she reproved herself. Why should it matter that she'd had to reveal she was an unmarried mother? Lots of women were single parents nowadays; many deliberately chose to be. Why should the revelation have left her feeling so awkward?

Perhaps, she reflected sadly, because her single-parent status was not her own choice. Circumstances had dictated her situation, not personal preferences.

Despite the fact that her qualms about Emily's health had been subdued, Claire's anxieties merely seemed to take another twist.

She paced restlessly round Emily's cot, frequently glancing out of the window towards the car park beyond.

How much had Alexandra told Brett when he'd got back to Sandwood last night? she wondered. How much of her own particular brand of poison had she dropped in his ear?

He'd stayed at the hospital until very late, waiting until Emily was settled in the ward before finally leaving, but Claire had no doubt that Alexandra would have waited up for him, determined to spill everything.

Every sense was on the alert for Brett's arrival and her nerves froze each time brisk footsteps sounded in the corridor.

'Would you like me to get you a cup of tea? It might help you relax a little,' one of the nurses kindly offered, sensing her tension.

Claire shook her head. 'No—thank you.' Her stomach was so knotted that she doubted she could eat or drink a thing.

'Mr Jarrett telephoned a little while ago. He'll probably be here soon,' the nurse informed her, clearly assuming the news would be both welcome and reassuring.

Claire jerked like a puppet whose strings had just been roughly tugged. 'Mr Jarrett phoned? When? How soon will he be here?'

'Very soon, I'm sure,' the nurse soothed. 'He sounded very concerned.'

Achieving just that right note of solicitude must have demanded all his acting skills, Claire thought on a wave of bitterness, for surely 'concern' was hardly the right word to describe Brett's mood right now.

Furious, enraged, murderous even, would surely have been more accurate?

She doubted very much that he would even begin to understand why she had kept the truth from him. He would see only her deception and dissimulation and none of the dreadful fears which had dictated her behaviour.

He would feel the pain of knowing that the agonising blank months missing from his life could have been lessened by her disclosure of the truth, but not her pain of knowing herself rejected and abandoned by him.

He would know the loss of missing the first six months of his daughter's life, but not her terrible dread of losing her daughter forever.

He would be acutely aware of the hurts she had inflicted on him, by omission if not by deed, but unaware of one iota of the misery he had inflicted on her.

In her mind, Brett's sense of rage and injustice grew to such proportions that by the time he appeared at the entrance to the children's ward she was racked with the most appalling fears. Only the knowledge that they were in a public place and that he could not attack her here kept her from racing coward-like in the opposite direction.

Her gaze flickered anxiously over his face, searching for the evidence that would confirm her own dread, and found instead tired lines etched round the startling blue of his eyes, suggesting he'd had as little sleep as she had.

His dark gaze settled on her briefly, taking in the taut lines of her body and the nervous tension which made her look like a terrified animal poised for flight.

Immediately his concern honed in on Emily. 'What's the matter? Is she——?'

'No,' Claire denied quickly, realising how perceptively he'd picked up on her own forebodings but misinterpreted them. 'Emily's fine. You were right. Just a virus, the consultant thinks. Nothing serious.'

A more adequate, fuller explanation was beyond her jittery power of expression right now. Hugging her arms to her, she turned away from him.

Had Alexandra told him? It seemed inconceivable that she hadn't, but, if he did know, Brett was delivering an

Oscar-winning performance of dissimulation. Where was the furious outburst she had been expecting?

Meanwhile Emily had noticed Brett's arrival and was now clambering to the side of the cot to bestow the adoring smile she seemed to reserve just for him.

'That little girl certainly thinks the world of her daddy,' one of the nurses commented smilingly as she passed by, the look she slid Brett not entirely without its own element of feminine appreciation.

Claire's hands clenched convulsively together as the world seemed to rock beneath her feet. If not Alexandra, then everyone else seemed intent on informing Brett of his part in Emily's existence.

'Take it easy.' Brett's arm slid round her trembling shoulders, making the tremor extend to the whole of her body. 'It's really not so terrible.'

Yes, it is, Claire longed to say, and you'll think so too when you realise it's not just an idle assumption, but the truth.

Her body ached with tiredness and the urge to lean back into Brett's solid strength was almost overwhelming. She longed to feel his hands wrapped around her, to feel herself embraced within the powerful circle of his arms.

Resisting that fierce yearning was unbelievably painful and Claire struggled to move away, fighting the pull of her need for him.

She smoothed shaky fingers over her hair, belatedly realising that she hadn't even combed it this morning, and shook the creases from last night's skirt.

'H-how's Alexandra?' she ventured, knowing that sooner or later she must ask the unavoidable question.

Brett studied her across the top of Emily's cot, his black-fringed gaze fully aware of her nervousness in posing the question at all.

'She's gone,' he said steadily. 'She'd already left when I returned to Sandwood last night. She ordered a taxi and caught the late train to London.'

Relief fell like a heavy shower over Claire. Alexandra had gone...without speaking to Brett. *He doesn't know*! That single thought stormed her mind, pushing all else aside.

In the end, pride must have proved a stronger force even than revenge. She'd told Brett she wouldn't be there when he got back and, knowing the battle to keep him was lost, she had kept that promise and at least retreated with some dignity intact.

Soberingly she realised that Brett was still watching her, seeing her all too evident relief play over her features. She couldn't be sorry that Alexandra had gone, but perhaps such unconcealed relief was a little insensitive in the circumstances. Although he'd said last night that the engagement was over, had he really meant it? 'Your engagement . . .'

A dull flush of colour highlighted the angle of his cheekbones. 'I told you. There was no engagement.'

Not now, maybe, but there had been one. Raw pain filled Claire's stomach as she recalled her conversation with Alexandra. *'I'm his fiancée. You were just some cheap tramp he picked up and then discarded.'*

As his fiancée, Alexandra had been privy to the letters she'd sent him. Claire could never forgive him for that betrayal; the wound went too deep.

'Not now, maybe——'

'There never was one,' Brett denied starkly. 'Alexandra had a long talk with Elspeth before she left. She admitted that there never had been any engagement. She made it up after learning I was suffering from amnesia. It was all a hoax...a hoax which Alexandra hoped would become reality.'

It sounded so incredulous that Claire could only stare at him. 'A hoax?'

'Apparently so.'

'But surely she knew you would realise it wasn't true?'

'How?' Brett gritted angrily. 'When you recover from a coma and are suffering from amnesia, you have to rely on other people's accounts to fill in the gaps in your own memory. You trust them to be honest. You don't think they will use those gaps to their own advantage. When Alexandra flaunted a ring at me and told me we had become engaged shortly before the accident, of course I was surprised. I had no recollection of our relationship having been that close or even intimate, but equally I had no reason to believe she would lie to me about something of such importance. So for a time I went along with it. That was my mistake. I knew instinctively that something was wrong but I did nothing about it.'

Claire's fingers tightened on the bars of Emily's cot, the knuckles whitening. Alexandra had deceived Brett into believing they were engaged! It was incredible but true. Her thoughts raced wildly as she conjectured what other deceptions Alexandra might have instrumented.

The letters! Could Alexandra have been lying about them too? But how? They had gone directly to Brett's home address. How could she have known about them unless he had told her? Except perhaps if she had seen them at his apartment and read them secretly without his knowledge?

It was one explanation at least and far less painful than the one Alexandra had offered, but it still didn't explain why, after receiving her letters, Brett had repeatedly failed to contact her.

She closed her eyes, trying to reconcile the warring factions inside her; every instinct told her that Brett would never have callously ignored the appeals those letters contained, but reason could construct no other explanation for his silence.

'Are you all right?'

Claire opened her eyes and nodded. 'J-just a little shocked, that's all.'

Then startled colour rose in her cheeks. After all, what right did she have to be shocked by anything Alexandra had done? Was it really any more incredible or deceitful than what she was doing to Brett? Where did honesty feature in her dealings with him?

Emily was his child and he didn't know it. Perhaps she hadn't kept the truth from him for cruel or selfish reasons, but she had deceived him none the less.

Brett reached over the top of the cot, his fingers closing on her white knuckles, melting her very bones.

'So was I at first,' he admitted softly. 'Then it began to make a crazy kind of sense. I knew all along there was something wrong. When Elspeth told me what Alexandra had said, a lot of missing pieces fell into place.'

Claire's eyes opened wide. 'P-pieces missing from your memory?'

'Not everything. But it's coming back.'

So she had a deadline. Either she told Brett the truth or risked him remembering for himself. Instinctively she knew that his reaction to the latter would be very different and far, far worse.

She had to be the one to tell him, and soon, but a public hospital ward was hardly the place for such confessions.

By Monday evening, Claire was worn out trying to keep a now very lively and very normal Emily amused. Frustrated by the confines of her hospital cot, Emily was stretching her mother's imagination to the limit trying to find new and varied distractions.

The results of the tests had taken longer to come through because there was only a skeleton staff in the laboratories over the Bank Holiday weekend. The test results were due the following morning.

Elspeth and Duncan had come to visit on the Sunday and again on the Monday afternoon, prior to travelling back to London. Given the difficulties of conducting a private conversation in such an environment, Elspeth had said little, only indicating how relieved she was that Brett and Alexandra were not to marry. Once or twice, though, Claire had caught her eyes on her and Emily, and had wondered just how much more Alexandra had told her than she had passed on to Brett.

When they left, Elspeth told Claire she would ring in a couple of days to 'check that everything was all right.' Claire couldn't help wondering if Elspeth was offering her some sort of time limit for telling Brett the truth.

Raw panic gripped her at the prospect. A childhood spent restraining the outpourings of normal human feelings had not prepared her well for such an encounter.

Eloquent speech was not her forte. She felt badly ill-equipped to try to explain to Brett the paralysing combination of fears and conjectures which had led to her decision not to tell him the truth from the beginning.

But tell him she knew she must.

For the last forty-eight hours, Brett had been a tower of strength, spending most of his waking hours at the hospital, offering her his support, and sharing the difficult task of keeping Emily entertained.

It was he now who offered to stay with Emily during her last night in hospital while Claire returned to Sandwood for a decent night's sleep.

'No, I couldn't.' Claire shook her head vigorously, unable to explain how watching Brett's affectionately relaxed handling of Emily during the last couple of days had almost torn her heart in two.

She too had got caught up in the enchanting interplay between father and daughter and, like the hospital staff, had almost come to believe it was true. She didn't know how she would bear it if, after everything, Brett should not want to acknowledge Emily as his. Leaving Emily to his charge tonight demanded a trust in the future she didn't yet dare to have.

'I don't know why *either* of you is planning to stay,' the ward sister, a motherly Irish woman in her mid-forties, interjected, stopping by Emily's cot. 'The best thing both of you can do for that wee lassie tonight is to go home and get a good night's rest. Look at her. She's not going to stir till morning and, if she does wake, she's enough charm to raise the wee folk. She'll not go short of attention.'

Emily was indeed fast asleep and looked certain of staying that way all night, lying on her back, her fist curled into a round ball against her cheek.

Watching her sleeping, Claire suddenly realised how incredibly tired she was and how appealing the sister's suggestion was. After two unsettled nights on the camp bed, the pull of her own bed and a comfortable night's sleep were strong. But only if Brett left too.

Seeing Claire's indecision, the sister urged Brett, 'Get this lassie home to her bed. And don't worry, I'll give you a ring if you're needed.'

Claire was too tired to protest when Brett's arm circled her shoulders, leading her towards the doorway, and by the time he had settled her into the front passenger seat of his Range Rover she was already half asleep.

After two days of lick 'n' promise washes at the hospital, the shower felt wonderful. Coupled with the half-hour catnap on the journey home from the hospital, it seemed incredibly refreshing. Earlier she felt as if she could sleep for a week, now she felt wide awake.

Liberally anointed with talc and perfume to take away the lingering aroma of hospital disinfectant, she pulled a silky nightie over her head and then slipped her arms into a fluffy towelling robe, tugging the belt tightly round her waist.

Bereft of make-up, damp hair slicked back on her head, she crept downstairs to the kitchen and Brett; while she'd showered, he'd offered to make some coffee and supper.

After the weekend, the house felt oddly quiet and the
noise of every creaking floorboard seemed magnified so
that by the time Claire reached the kitchen it sounded
as if the equivalent of a ten-gun salute had announced
her arrival. Was it that which accounted for the surge
of colour which swept through her cheeks as she opened
the door?

Brett had his back to her and through the silky material of his shirt she watched the play of whipcord
muscles flexing over wide shoulders, then followed their
line to the narrow waist, lean hips, and finally long,
muscular thighs.

Moments before, the percolating coffee and toasted
cheese sandwiches had smelt tantalisingly appetising, but
now all desire for refreshment vanished and Claire was
filled with a wave of longing so fierce that it nearly made
her gasp.

Indeed she must have made some sound for Brett
swung round to face her, his dark gaze travelling over
her flushed features and then down over the feminine
curves visible beneath her robe.

Neither of them said a word. Indeed speech seemed
entirely superfluous as Brett easily bridged the gap between them and gathered her into his arms. His mouth
dropped to bury itself hotly at the sensitive spot where
her throat disappeared into the towelling V of her robe,
and Claire's legs almost gave way beneath her.

His arms went round her then, supporting her weight
against him as his mouth ravished the tender flesh of
her neck and shoulders.

By the time his mouth reached hers, her arms were
wound around his shoulders, her fingers entwining in

the springy thickness of his hair, meeting the fierce heat of his mouth with equal need. There was an almost savage urgency in the lips crushed against hers and in the tongue which penetrated deep into the soft recesses of her mouth, sucking in the essence of her like a man falling on a spring of fresh water in the middle of a desert.

But if he drank from her then she took sustenance from him too, her tongue entwining with his in an erotic snake dance, feeling it graze the tender recesses of her mouth in sweet, hard lashes.

'God, I want you so much,' he admitted roughly, his mouth even now skimming along her jaw and dipping into the sensitive hollows of her throat, as if her skin were like some once tasted narcotic which he had been deprived of for too long.

'I want you too,' Claire admitted breathlessly, air quivering in tormented gasps in her throat. 'But first we must talk...'

'No.' Brett shook his head on the whispered growl. 'We can talk later. I need you. Now.'

His admission was a powerful aphrodisiac in itself, rousing her own need to new, giddy heights and easily crushing the tentative words she had been trying to formulate in her mind. Later...yes...later they could talk.

Effortlessly he lifted her into his arms and carried her up the stairs and along the corridor to his bedroom, each step accompanied by a silky promise which sent the blood soaring through her veins in erotic response.

Expert fingers dropped to the sash of her robe, tugging it loose and then easing the towelling covering from her shoulders.

Had she unconsciously chosen this nightgown because she knew what was going to happen? Claire wondered on a last wing of sanity. A diaphanous, silky affair with boot-lace straps, it had nothing practical to recommend it at all, but it was incredibly lovely and it made her feel deliciously feminine.

As the robe slid from her, Brett's gaze raked over her, as explicit as any caress, exploring the proud swelling of her breasts, the feminine curve of her hips, and finally the dark tangle of curls at the joining of her thighs.

'You're so beautiful,' he murmured thickly, cupping one hand round the slender column of her throat and drawing her to him while the other went to curve possessively over one swollen breast. His thumb grazed a taut nipple and his mouth swooped to capture the soft gasps which rose in her throat, arching her fluidly against him and letting her feel the hard male power of him in a heated thrust against her thighs.

Molten and fluid, Claire tumbled back on to the bed, pulling Brett with her. His full weight pressed against her and his mouth felt hot and hard as it moved over hers, dropping lower and lower until it brushed the nightgown aside and captured one taut nipple, suckling and teasing it until Claire arched beneath him, whimpering her need in a series of increasingly erotic demands.

The fingers of his other hand plucked at the straining nipple of her neglected breast, playing it until it too strained impatiently beneath his touch, making Claire writhe in urgent need.

Then impatiently the gown was tugged over her head and Brett was removing his own clothing, barely aided by Claire's trembling fingers. Yet for all that she couldn't take her eyes off him; her gaze devoured the hard male contours and angles like a person starved, as indeed she had been starved for fifteen long months.

He was beautiful, superbly male, physical perfection.

'You want me every bit as much as I want you, don't you?'

The rasped demand was intensely primitive, intensely arousing, and Claire nodded, her mouth suddenly dry with love and passion.

But not for long, for Brett's tongue was hot and wet as it drove fiercely into her mouth and his body was hard and demanding as it lowered on to hers, grinding against her thighs in enticing circles until they relaxed against the velvet brush of his maleness.

Every nerve in her body felt raw, every vein stretched to its full capacity as the blood pounded through her, lifting her to a fever pitch of desire. Every inch of her was alert to the tormenting length of his body as it rocked against hers, the abrasive roughness of his chest against her sensitised nipples, the slick strength of rippling muscles tensing beneath her roaming fingers, the solid length of his thighs as they skilfully parted hers.

His teasing thrusts went on and on until she could bear it no longer and her body arched blindly against him, demanding and begging that he should release her from the tortures he was inflicting. Her own control was being stretched to its limits and suddenly she twisted beneath him in savage, protesting torment, fingernails raking his back lower and lower until her hands locked on to his body, drawing him to her.

Her sobbing moan told him of her need and suddenly his own control was shattering. His hands curved hard against her hips as he rose above her, then drove into her with a hot, piercing insistence that pushed her closer and closer to the edge of the world. Nothing else existed except that brink which she must reach ... now within her sight, now within her grasp.

A final, searing thrust sent her spiralling over it, tumbling into infinity on wave after wave of the most sublime delight, distantly grasping Brett's own rough groan of male satisfaction as he fell into oblivion with her.

Satiated and utterly fulfilled, Claire stretched like a contented cat against Brett's body and fell into a deep, blissful sleep.

CHAPTER NINE

WHEN Claire woke next morning, sunlight was streaming through the window where the curtains remained undrawn, and Brett was no longer beside her.

For a few seconds, she stretched languorously, savouring the sensation of warm heaviness which filled her body, making her feel utterly satiated and totally contented, then her eyes caught sight of the alarm clock.

Nearly ten-thirty! It couldn't be! The clock must be wrong. Surely it was only around six?

Snatching up her robe from beside the bed, she pulled it round her and raced along the corridor to her own room, only to have her own bedside alarm smugly confirm Brett's.

Her first thought was that she should have been at the hospital collecting Emily by now. The second, following close on its heels, was to wonder where Brett was and why he had allowed her to sleep so late.

Pulling on her robe properly, she secured the belt tightly round her waist and then disappeared back into the corridor and down the stairs, taking them two at a time.

Brett's probably in the kitchen, fixing breakfast, she thought breathlessly. He hasn't realised the time ... he doesn't know I should be at the hospital ... she repeated over and over again like some well-rehearsed litany.

But when she reached the kitchen there was no sign of Brett, no sign even that he'd been there since last night. The coffee percolator had switched itself off, and the rich, dark liquid inside it was stone-cold. Limp toasted sandwiches lay unappetisingly on plates, untouched and forgotten.

Don't panic, Claire intoned softly to herself, fighting down waves of fear. There has to be a simple explanation.

The back door was locked, its key still in it, so Brett hadn't gone outside. She raced back to the bottom of the stairs and called his name, but it echoed hollowly back at her, unanswered.

Really frightened by now, she wrenched open the front door and stared at the empty place in the garage where Brett's Range Rover should have been.

He's gone! The pronouncement spun round and round inside her mind, like a Catherine wheel gaining momentum with every twirling circuit.

A horrible, empty sensation filled her stomach as she gazed at the empty space. But where had he gone?

A note! He must have left a note! Frantically she slammed the door shut behind her and raced through the house searching for some scrap of paper that would give her a clue to his whereabouts...beside the phone, in the kitchen, on the bedside cabinet. Nothing!

Claire made her way back down the stairs and slumped heavily on the bottom step as her legs seemed to turn to jelly beneath her.

Brett knew!

She didn't question the rightness of her conclusion because she knew instinctively that it was the correct one. Their lovemaking had been the catalyst which had bridged the gaps between Brett's hazy memories and cold, hard reality.

He hadn't learned the truth with the gentle sensitivity she'd planned, but with a brutal slap in the face. And now he'd gone.

Emily! Claire struggled upright. She must go and collect Emily. The ward staff would be wondering why she was so late.

On legs that felt hardly able to support her, she struggled through to the kitchen and dialled the hospital, quickly getting through to the children's ward.

'It's Emily's mother here ... I ... I just wanted to let you know that I'm on my way to collect her ... I'm sorry——'

'That's all right,' the ward sister interrupted her cheerfully. 'Emily's father picked her up about half an hour ago.'

Claire didn't hear any more. That single sentence filled her mind and blocked out everything else. Brett had got Emily. The terrifying nightmare had become reality.

Numb fingers set the receiver back in its cradle and she slid weakly into a chair, barely able to move for the paralysing fear which gripped her. She knew she should be doing something, but what?

The police! She should contact the police. Frozen fingers reached for the telephone buttons and then stilled. How seriously would they take her complaint? After all, she'd allowed the assumption that Brett was Emily's father to go uncorrected; she'd given the hospital staff no reason to think she would be concerned about Brett collecting Emily in her place.

Alerting the police now seemed a belated display of caution, like the proverbial shutting of the stable door after the horse had bolted.

She could phone Duncan and Elspeth. They would surely stop Brett doing anything rash. She was scrabbling through the book, looking for their number, when the front door slammed shut with a loud, ominous bang, making Claire's whole body shake. Moments later, Brett appeared in the doorway, Emily in his arms.

The relief at seeing them was almost overwhelming, yet instinctively her first concern was for Emily's well-being.

'The tests?'

'Were all clear.'

Her arms ached to hold Emily; she longed to reach out for her. Yet there was something in the possessive way Brett held her that said he would not relinquish her easily. Fear, like bitter gall, rose in her throat.

'Y-you're not going to take her away from me, are you?' she stammered, terrified by that possibility.

'Is that what you thought?' Brett demanded coldly. 'That I would do to you what you have done to me and keep *our* child from you?'

Claire swallowed convulsively. 'Brett, please, I know how it must look.'

'Do you?' he demanded with controlled fury. 'We've been living together in this house for ten days. *Ten* days! And on any one of them you could have told me the truth. Yet instead you chose to persist with the most appalling lie. And not just one lie. Many. You used my loss of memory to your own advantage, playing me along in some pathetic little game you had concocted for your pleasure. And to think *you* had the gall to be shocked by what Alexandra had done.'

Claire shook her head. 'It wasn't like that.'

'Wasn't it? Then what other name do you give this pastime of yours? This pathetic little practice of pretending to be a complete stranger to a man whose lover you once were and who is the father of your child?'

She shook violently. 'You're twisting what happened.'

'No, quite the opposite,' Brett insisted coldly. 'I am only now beginning to untangle the ugly twisted mess you created. Memory is very strange. Other senses can sometimes be more powerful than sight. Touch...smell...hearing. Last night, when I held you naked in my arms as you drifted off to sleep, you murmured my name, your scent was all around me, and I suddenly knew...*knew* then that it was not the first time I'd held you so intimately. All at once I realised the truth yet I could not believe it. My memory of our time in Sydney was crystal-clear and yet still I would not believe it. It was beyond my power of credulity to comprehend how anyone could cheat and lie so despicably. And yet that is precisely what you have done, isn't it?'

'No!' The denial was forced from a throat as dry as parchment. 'I wanted to tell you but I...I didn't know how at first. You didn't know me. How could I just have blurted out the truth?'

'The truth would surely have been no more difficult to "blurt out" than the lies you spewed in such abundance,' Brett said ruthlessly, his expression as taut and lashing as a whip frozen in motion.

'The lies only started after I became afraid to tell you the truth,' Claire whispered, struggling to face Brett's

brooding rage. 'I didn't know how you would react...
I was terrified of telling you for fear of what you would
do.'

Brett's mouth hardened derisively. 'I don't believe
what I'm hearing. You have the nerve to sit there and
tell me it's *my* fault you were forced to lie to me?'

'N-not your fault, no,' Claire stammered. 'You
couldn't know how some of the things you said
frightened me... Your views on single parents... I knew
you thought my circumstances made it impossible for
me to raise a child properly and I was terrified that you
might try to take Emily from me if you knew the truth.'

'My God!' Brett drawled furiously. 'You took every
word I uttered, twisted it out of context, and took it on
yourself to act as judge, jury and executioner. I was con-
victed without ever being given the opportunity to say
a word in my own defence.'

'No!' Claire denied, begging him to understand. 'I
was going to tell you the truth. I tried last night... I
thought this morning——'

'This morning?' It was a bellow of disgusted rage. 'I
have a six-month-old daughter and you decide to tell me
this morning!'

Claire raked a hand across her forehead, pushing back
a tumble of hair in an anguished gesture. 'I tried to tell
you fifteen months ago,' she said desperately. 'I wanted
to tell you. That's why I wrote. I wrote to you over and
over again asking you to contact me. You never did.'

'Don't lie,' Brett gritted harshly. 'You left Australia
without a word of explanation. It was only through contacting the airline that I knew you'd gone at all. You

disappeared like some phantom in the night. No word. No explanation. Nothing.'

'That's not true,' Claire denied vigorously. 'I wrote you a letter, telling you my mother was ill and that I had to get back to England. After I got home I must have written you a dozen letters. You never answered any of them. You received them, I know you did, because Alexandra told me about them.'

Brett's eyes narrowed to two chinks of blue. 'Alexandra said I'd received letters from you?'

Claire nodded. 'Yes.'

'It's not possible.' Brett shook his head. 'There were no letters.'

'Yes, there were. Alexandra had seen them... She knew I was staying in Yorkshire with my parents. How could she have known about that if she hadn't read the letters?' The words tumbled out in quick succession.

Brett paced to and fro, then stopped, one hand holding Emily, the other clenching tightly on a chair back, his expression so full of anger that the chair seemed merely a substitute for her neck. 'Where did you send them?'

'To your home address, of course,' Claire said, adding quietly, 'Where else could I send them? I didn't even know your telephone number or where you worked. You never told me about your links with Atlas Engineering or your relationship with Duncan, remember?'

With a wave of his hand, Brett dismissed the latter and homed in instead on the former assertion, the taut lines of his face hardening into a frown. 'When I was away, my home mail was automatically redirected to the office, and I was away a lot after you'd gone. Most of my mail would have gone through the office.'

'And through Alexandra?' Claire suddenly saw how easy it would have been for Alexandra to divert any letters she didn't want Brett to see.

'Yes.'

Alexandra could simply have read the letters and then destroyed them. Brett would never have known about them. 'You never got my letters...any of them?'

'No,' Brett agreed harshly. 'None of them.'

Claire's teeth bit painfully into her lower lip as she contemplated the significance of this development. For her it changed everything; from believing herself abandoned by Brett, she now realised they had both been victims of Alexandra's trickery and scheming.

Just as Alexandra had intended him to, Brett had believed it was *she* who had left him, returning to England without a word, leaving no forwarding address, not contacting him.

But if he had only been honest with her from the start, told her of his links with Atlas Engineering, his relationship with Duncan, those misunderstandings would never have arisen. She could have contacted him directly.

'Why didn't you tell me that you were Duncan's brother?'

'What?' Brett seemed engrossed in his own thoughts. 'Oh, that!' He shrugged. 'It was never intended to be a secret. When you told me that first night that you worked for Duncan, I thought it might erect a barrier between us if you knew I was his brother. It was refreshing to meet someone who knew nothing about me, who accepted me at face value for what I was, not who I was. I didn't want to spoil that and so, for a while, I put those

details aside. I planned to tell you when you returned
to Sydney, but, of course, you never did return.'

'I couldn't help that,' Claire protested, stunned by the
discovery of such a simple explanation behind the omis-
sions when she had weaved all manner of deliberate
duplicities to account for them. 'My mother was ill. I
had to return to England as quickly as possible.'

Cool blue eyes fixed her in their sights. 'So you say.'

'It's true.'

Brett's mouth twisted. 'True? That's an odd word
coming from you. I wonder if you even understand its
meaning.'

Tears brimmed in Claire's eyes. 'That's not fair. Can
you imagine how I felt the day you arrived and I discovered who you were? I was stunned. I had no idea
what to do.'

'So you decided to do nothing.'

'I decided to wait,' Claire sobbed.

'And then lie.'

'No!'

Brett arched a jet brow in contempt. 'No? Let us at
last be honest with each other. I understand you felt betrayed by me. You had written to me and I had not responded. You were as unaware of Alexandra's
interference as I was. On the evidence, I appeared to
have abandoned you and our child. Then, out of nowhere, I arrived once again in your life. Except this time
the tables were turned. Instead of you being ignorant of
who I was, this time it was I who was ignorant of who
you were. You had an advantage over me and you decided to use it. You decided to get even for the pain you
had suffered. My punishment was to be kept in ig-

norance, not only of what we had been to each other, but, worst of all, of my child's existence. That is what I cannot forgive. You would not have told me Emily was mine.'

The thundering roar of that last charge turned Claire's cheeks ghostly white. 'I would, of course I would. I wanted to b-but I was frightened.'

'So you say,' Brett jeered.

'I was terrified you would try to take her away from me if you knew...terrified you would try to get custody of her.'

'Am I expected to believe this? You're an intelligent woman. Did you really believe the British courts would award custody to me, an unmarried father, a man who wasn't even aware of her existence for the first six months of her life, in preference to you, the child's mother? Was that likely?'

Claire was shaking uncontrollably now. 'N-not likely, maybe, but I didn't know if it was possible. You have money, influence...and you were shortly to be married. I thought a court might feel you had more to offer than I did... I even thought you might try to take Emily to Australia. I wasn't thinking straight, don't you understand? I was frightened,' she pleaded with him for understanding.

But there was not one iota of sympathy or compassion in Brett's black gaze as he glared down at her. 'All I understand right now is that you lied to me about something which you had no right—no right at all—to lie to me about. My child,' he said with slow, chilling deliberation.

Claire's fingers pleated the belt of her robe through a blur of tears. She too understood one thing at least. Right now Brett was furiously angry with her, far too angry to absorb one half of the explanation she was trying to offer him. All he knew at this moment was his own rage, his own bitter sense of deprivation at his ignorance of Emily's existence, and both were too great right now to admit any chink of understanding for what she too had gone through.

What had been so beautiful last night was now damaged beyond repair. If only she'd told Brett the truth then, as she had planned, perhaps his reaction would have been different...muted at least. If only...if only... Life was full of 'if only's and they were always far more beguiling than cold, hard reality. The future now was a murky fog which she dreaded entering.

There was just one thing she needed to know. 'Y-you won't take Emily away from me, will you?'

Brett's mouth curved in a hard, humourless smile. 'Don't worry! My thirst for revenge isn't quite as deep as yours. I have no intention of doing to you what you did to me. You're Emily's mother. She needs you. I know that.'

A painful gulp of relief caught in Claire's throat. Thank God Brett was at least prepared to acknowledge that. Guilt gnawed at her stomach as she wondered if she hadn't been very unjust in thinking he wouldn't. If Emily had to be the child of a single parent, then at least he accepted the parent should be her, not him. Her voice came out far more wobbly than she intended. 'Can I hold her—now?'

'You can...just as soon as you agree to my terms,' Brett intoned smoothly.

'Terms?'

'Only one, really. Marriage.'

'Marriage?' Claire mimicked stupidly.

One jet brow arched sardonically. 'What else did you expect?'

'But you said you'd give Emily back to me... You admitted that she needed me.'

Black-fringed eyes glittered down at her. 'So she does, but that doesn't mean she needs a father less. Whatever else my child may lack, she will at least have that need fulfilled.'

Claire's hands fluttered in a confused gesture. 'But...but marriage? We can both be Emily's parents without marriage.'

Brett's expression was chillingly intransigent. 'No, we can't,' he contradicted her icily. 'I will not have my daughter brought up in the midst of some modern arrangement of separated parents living in separate homes with an assortment of step-parents coming in and out of her life. My child will not know that kind of insecurity and uncertainty. For Emily's sake, you and I *will* be married and we will stay married.'

Once Claire had longed to hear Brett say those words, but now he made them sound like a life-sentence, entirely devoid of love. What kind of marriage would they have, entered into in such circumstances? Old-fashioned in some respects and modern in others?

Alexandra's words came back to her. *'Brett will never be faithful to one woman.'* Would Claire be expected to adopt a 'modern' attitude to Brett's infidelities, accepting them as the price she must pay for marriage to her child's father?

'And...and if I don't want that kind of marriage?' she managed shakily.

'You have no choice,' Brett told her brutally. 'Neither have I. The choice was made for us the moment Emily was conceived.' He paused, smouldering eyes settling on her pooling eyes and trembling mouth. 'That's my condition. If you choose not to accept it, then I will fight you for Emily and, believe me, I will win. As you said, I have money and I have influence, and I will not hesitate to use both to achieve what I want.'

The chilling certainty of that last assertion froze the marrow in Claire's bones. 'You're right. You don't leave me any choice,' she conceded in an undertone.

'Good! I'm glad we are agreed on that, at least.'

They stared at each other, Brett's ferocious gaze daring her to contradict him. She didn't. In numbed shock, her mind veered completely from the bleak future he was offering—no, not offering, demanding—to focus on the most mundane banality of the present. Her fingers plucked nervously at the gaping V of her gown, as she belatedly realised she was still naked beneath it.

'I-I'd better go and get dressed,' she murmured.

Brett's gaze flicked to the exposed swell of her breasts and then away again, eyes darkening briefly, 'Yes, you better had,' he drawled roughly. 'I'll contact Duncan and Elspeth and then you can phone your parents to let them know about the wedding. I want everything arranged as quickly as possible.'

As he spoke, Claire stood up, then felt a wave of dizziness wash over her. Afterwards she didn't know if it was caused by the fact that she hadn't eaten since yesterday afternoon or by Brett's words. White knuckles came into sudden contact with the hard surface of the table.

'Are you all right?' Instantly Brett was in front of her, one hand closing on her shoulder to support her.

She nodded weakly then, contrarily, shook her head. 'My parents... It's going to be difficult. I haven't been in touch with them for nearly thirteen months.'

'Why? Did you turn your back on them as well?'

That last insolent taunt drew a spurt of bitter anger. 'No, I did not,' Claire retorted. 'When I told them I was pregnant, they gave me an ultimatum. Either I had an abortion or they didn't wish to see me again. As far as I was concerned there was no choice. I couldn't have had an abortion.'

Brett paled visibly. 'My God! Your own parents demanded that?'

'That's right.' Claire nodded, hugging her arms to her as a sudden chill engulfed her at the memory. A lump rose in her throat and she had difficulty speaking. 'My mother didn't want the product of "some sordid little affair" foisted on her as her grandchild.'

One hand came up to cup her chin, tilting her face to his. 'What we had wasn't sordid,' he said with surprising gentleness.

Hot tears pressed against the backs of Claire's eyes and she blinked rapidly. 'In my mother's eyes it was. We weren't married and you weren't around when I discovered I was pregnant.'

'But now I am around,' Brett said deliberately, staring down at her, watching the play of emotions on her face.

'And soon we will be married. I think it's about time I met your parents and made them aware of both those facts.'

The huge country hotel on the outskirts of her home village was the ultimate in elegance and luxury. As a child, Claire had passed it almost daily on her way to school, never dreaming she would ever stay there.

It had taken just over three hours to pack suitcases and drive to north Yorkshire, finally drawing into the drive of the hotel at nearly three-thirty.

Brett took care of the booking arrangements while Claire stood awkwardly near the information rack, Emily in her arms, ostensibly examining the rows of literature on the area.

Had Brett booked one room or two? she wondered anxiously now, following the porter who carried their luggage towards the lift.

She wanted to ask Brett, but he seemed very cool and remote, and besides, a confined lift with a porter in attendance was hardly the place to be discussing their sleeping arrangements.

In fact, Brett had taken a whole suite. There was a sitting-room, with wonderful views over the moors, a large bedroom with a huge brass bedstead, which Claire's eyes skimmed over hastily, a bathroom and a smaller bedroom for Emily.

'I'll arrange for the cot to be brought up as soon as possible,' the porter said as he left, pleased with the generous tip he had received from Brett and disposed to be as helpful as possible.

'Do you like it?'

Claire was standing at the window, her back to Brett, gazing out over the vast sweep of open moorland where grouse and pheasant ranged.

'It's lovely,' she conceded quietly, privately wondering if the kind of expensive luxuries Brett would introduce her to could compensate for the loveless marital arrangement they would share, and knew they couldn't.

Brett took Emily from her arms, his eyes lighting up with the first genuine warmth she had seen all day as his daughter smiled at him.

Brett might be wrong about a great many things, but he was right about one thing at least: Emily did deserve all that he could give her, not just the material things, but the love as well. And Claire had no doubt that he did love her. It was there, for everyone to see, when he looked at her.

If only it was there for me as well, Claire thought on a faint pang of envy for her daughter. Last night she had been sure it was, or could be, but today had all but wiped out any such hopes.

At the moment Brett was totally enmeshed in his own pain and resentment over what had happened. Perhaps, she thought, if she had been able to express her own fears and anxieties more clearly, if she had been more articulate in making Brett understand the dilemmas she had faced, he would have understood her actions better. But in that she seemed to have failed completely.

Brett was convinced she had kept silent out of some bitter desire for revenge, deliberately allowing his loss of memory to be perpetuated for warped reasons of her own. She could only hope that when that initial shock of discovering the truth had gone he would view her behaviour a little more dispassionately and a little less critically.

'Why don't you telephone your parents and tell them you're here?' Brett suggested.

It was one of the most difficult telephone calls that Claire had ever had to make. Her father answered the telephone; he was clearly surprised to hear her voice and, being unprepared, sounded even more stilted and formal than usual. Already worn out by the events of the day, Claire felt her own natural warmth shrivel during the awkward exchange.

'I'm staying in the area and thought I might come and see you,' she explained.

'Oh!'

'I-I've got some news for you.'

'I see.'

'When can I call?'

There was a heavy silence, then, 'Best to come when the shop's shut.'

Of course! The demands of the shop invariably came before everything else. 'Tonight, then? After you've closed?'

'Ay, that'll do,' her father agreed in his bluff Yorkshire accent.

Arrangements made, she set the receiver down and turned to find Brett watching her.

'You didn't mention Emily... or me,' he prompted.

Claire bit her lip. 'He didn't ask.'

'When will you learn that you can't avoid difficult issues simply by not talking about them?' Brett demanded, brutally cutting into defences already desperately weakened by the events of the last forty-eight hours. 'Keeping silent does not make them go away. I should have thought you would have learned that by now.'

'It's difficult to unlearn the habits of many years,' she said tautly, adding rawly, 'When I was growing up, my parents discouraged any discussion about real feelings or real needs. They didn't want to know. Everything had to be kept subdued and quiet, even emotions. That kind of repression becomes a habit that's hard to break.'

She fell silent, her own outburst shocking her a little and making her realise how rarely she gave rein to the true expression of her feelings. It was shocking, but it felt good as well, and she found herself wondering if she shouldn't try it more often.

Brett arranged a baby-sitter for Emily at the hotel, suggesting that to take her with them on the first visit might create additional pressures on a family reunion that already had the makings of a somewhat fraught event. Claire was secretly relieved; introducing Brett, who insisted on accompanying her, would be quite difficult enough without exposing Emily, the granddaughter they had never wanted, to her parents' critical appraisal.

When her father open the side-door to the flat in response to their knock, he greeted Claire uncomfortably, with none of the affection most fathers and daughters shared, the sort of affection Claire wanted Emily and Brett to share. He shuffled awkwardly forward, finally shaking her hand in a cool, almost businesslike manner.

'This is Brett...Brett Jarrett,' Claire said quickly. 'We...we met in Australia.'

George Seymour had to look up to greet Brett and was obviously a little intimidated by this tall, assured-looking man at his daughter's side. 'Er—pleased...to—er—meet you, Mr Jarrett.'

'What Claire hasn't yet explained,' Brett added smoothly, 'is that I am Emily's father and that she and I are to be married as soon as possible.'

Claire flushed bright red to the roots of her hair at Brett's directness, faintly sympathetic to the realisation that he had also managed to rob her father of coherent speech with that stark announcement.

'Oh!' her father muttered, obviously at a loss for words. 'Well—er—do come in, Mr Jarrett. My wife will be—er—very pleased to hear that, I'm sure.'

Claire's mother was paler and thinner than she had been the last time Claire had seen her. The smile she greeted her daughter with seemed to have shrunk too. Barely evident, it was hardly encouraging.

'This is Mr Jarrett, Margaret,' George introduced Brett to his wife. 'Apparently he and Claire are to—er—to be married.'

Brett held out his hand. 'I'm also your granddaughter's father,' he said suavely, the silky edge to his voice daring a hostile response.

Claire, watching her mother's gaze flicker over the expensive lines of Brett's dark suit and glimpse the Cartier watch just visible beneath the white cuff of his shirt, knew there wouldn't be one. Brett was exactly the sort of 'decent man' her mother had always wanted for her. She would be delighted by the news.

'I can't understand why Claire didn't tell us about you earlier,' Margaret Seymour said.

'I understood she did,' Brett challenged coolly.

For a moment, Claire's mother looked uncomfortable. 'She mentioned a man, of course, but few details. If we'd known then...' Her voice trailed off.

Claire silently supplied the missing words; if they'd known Brett was wealthy and eligible and willing to marry her, their reaction would have been different. The question of an abortion would never have arisen.

'Of course when Claire told us that she'd written to you several times but that you hadn't replied, naturally we assumed that you...weren't interested.'

Unconsciously her mother confirmed what Claire had told him about all the letters she had sent.

Brett's fingers reached out to close over her stiff, unresponsive ones. 'There were some...difficulties which we needed to resolve,' he interposed smoothly.

Margaret's eyes darted anxiously from one to the other. 'But you are getting married?'

Brett's hand gripped Claire's so tightly that she thought the blood flow might be in danger. 'Of course, as soon as the necessary arrangements can be made,' he assured her. 'Naturally, you are both invited to the wedding.'

Claire watched Brett's lethal charm work on her parents, noted their exchanged glances of surprised pleasure that this was the man who was to marry their daughter, and knew that little had really changed. They were still more concerned with what appeared on the surface than what was happening beneath.

They were oblivious to her tension and anxieties, seeing
only what they wanted to see; that she had managed to
find herself an eminently suitable man for a husband.
More than that they really didn't want to know. The fact
that Brett didn't love her mattered not at all.

CHAPTER TEN

BACK at the hotel, the baby-sitter informed them that Emily had been 'as good as gold'. She'd woken once and had given the baby-sitter a quizzical look, but after a drink and a cuddle had gone back to sleep again.

'Thank you for keeping an eye on her. I don't usually leave her with people she doesn't know,' Claire explained, escorting her to the door. 'But it would have been difficult to take her with me tonight.'

'It was a pleasure,' the woman assured her, smiling. 'If you need my services again, just ask at Reception.'

In the meantime, Brett had gone to the well-stocked drinks cabinet and poured a generous measure of brandy into a glass. 'Would you like one?' he offered now as she closed the door.

Claire normally drank very little alcohol, but after the events of the day she felt in need of something restorative. She nodded. 'Thank you.'

Her body felt very tense and stiff, far too rigid to sit down, and so, cupping the glass between her fingers, she went to stand by the window again, looking out over the view she had surveyed earlier, shrouded in darkness now.

She and Brett had agreed to call on her parents again the following day, taking Emily with them. As family reunions went, it had hardly been brimming with warmth and affection, but she supposed it was a start.

At least Brett had had an opportunity to meet her parents for himself and perhaps understood a little better the atmosphere she had grown up in and the communication difficulties that had created. Maybe he would realise that it was, in part, a repressive cowardice bred over many years which had led to her keeping silent, not a deliberate act of retribution.

The sudden sensation of lean fingers burrowing into her hair and massaging the taut muscles in the back of her neck made her jump. The fingers stilled but didn't move away.

'You'll have to get used to referring to "we" and "us" when you talk about Emily,' Brett said gently. 'You're not a lone parent any more. There are two of us in Emily's life now.'

Frowning, Claire reviewed the brief exchange of words with the baby-sitter and realised she had talked about Emily as if she were still solely hers, solely her responsibility. She wasn't. From now on, she was going to have to get used to sharing both the problems and the pleasures of parenting with Brett.

Absorbed in contemplating the changes that would require, not just practical but emotional too, she took a gulp of brandy, too much, and felt it burn the back of her throat with its fiery heat.

Far more scorching though was the feel of Brett's fingers, moving once more over her skin. Unconsciously, she arched her neck a little to the side as his thumb discovered a particularly knotted muscle.

'It wasn't easy for you, was it?' he murmured softly.

'What wasn't?'

'Discovering you were pregnant . . . Dealing with your parents' reproach. What did you do after you left their home?'

The gentleness in his voice was so at variance with the steel rage it had been full of that morning that Claire found herself stammering in confusion.

'I-I went to Cornwall to stay with my Aunt Helen.'

'The same aunt who paid for your trip to Australia?'

He'd remembered, then! Claire nodded. 'The very one. I stayed there almost until Emily was born. She was wonderful to me. I could never repay her kindness. She helped me when I had no one else to turn to.'

There was a rough intake of breath, then, 'I'd like to meet her.'

'I think she'd like to meet you too,' Claire said and knew it was true. Aunt Helen and Brett would get on wonderfully well. They shared the same vibrancy and zest for living.

Abruptly the fingers which had been caressing her neck stopped and fell away. 'You must have thought I was a bastard. You must have hated me.'

The bitter demand vibrated harshly on her ear-drums and she turned slowly round to look at him then, seeing the pain he was inflicting on himself this time. Incredibly it hurt more than when he'd flagellated her that morning. Instinctively her fingers moved up to touch the hard line of his jaw.

She shook her head. 'No, I never thought that and I never hated you.' She paused, struggling to find the words to continue. 'I was desperately hurt because I thought you didn't care, but I never hated you. How could I? I loved you.'

She'd never said those words to him before; even in Sydney, although she'd known it was true, she'd been too insecure to venture them, scared that Brett might find such a declaration too possessive and restricting.

Speaking about feelings had never been easy for her, but now she had to because she knew Brett needed to hear it, knew he needed to know she didn't blame him for what had happened.

Brett's eyes were like glittering sapphires and his hands moved to her shoulders, gripping them in fists of iron. 'You loved me? Even when you thought you'd been abandoned to face the pregnancy alone? Even when your parents threw you out?'

Claire nodded. 'In a way I loved you more. Part of you was growing inside me. If I'd hated you, I would have been hating our child. Whatever happened, I could never have done that.'

Abruptly his hands fell from her shoulders and he twisted away, prowling round the room like some confined jungle cat. 'That only makes all the things I said to you this morning all the more unforgivable. Last night, after we made love, it was as if a curtain had dropped from before my eyes. It had been getting more and more transparent every day during the last ten days; each day I would see a little more of the elusive scenes playing out beyond it, but never clearly. Then last night, as I held you in my arms, everything returned. Meeting you in Sydney... spending the week together. I was going to propose, you know.... when I got back... That's what I planned.'

He tossed that last piece of information out as if it hardly mattered, but Claire caught it and held on to it as tightly as she might have done a pouch of priceless gems.

'But you weren't there,' Brett continued. 'There was no letter, no telephone call, no message. When I contacted the airline, I learned you had altered your flight and returned to England a few days earlier. I assumed you had done it deliberately because you'd decided to end our relationship and didn't have the guts to tell me to my face——'

'No, it wasn't like that——' Claire broke in urgently, but Brett lifted a silencing hand.

'Please, let me finish. I admit, I went off the rails. For the next couple of months I lived life like a madman. I hardly spent any time in Sydney, deliberately engineering trips to other parts of the country just to escape the painful memories you'd left behind. When I wasn't working, I was drinking, so that eventually much of my life became a blur. If that plane accident hadn't happened, then another sort would. I was asking for trouble. My life was lived permanently in the fast lane because to slow down meant thinking and remembering and that was precisely what I didn't want to do.'

Claire paled at the suicidal lifestyle Brett was describing. She'd had no idea of what *he'd* gone through, none at all. Had her loss really affected him so deeply?

'You have no idea the number of times I picked up the telephone to Duncan, wanting to ask him about you—where you were, what you were doing. But pride wouldn't let me. I reasoned that you'd walked out on me and that was the end of it. I wasn't going to chase you halfway round the world. If you wanted to, you could contact me. I didn't know then about Alexandra's bloody interference.'

His fist banged against the top of an oak cupboard. 'God! How I wish now I'd made that phone call. It would have spared both of us so much misery. When I came round after the plane crash, my whole life during that period was gone; I had no recollection of any of it. I suppose a psychiatrist would say that it was so painful, I'd blocked it out as a safety mechanism. Anyway, when Alexandra appeared with a ring on her finger, I just assumed she was telling me the truth. Deep down, I sensed that something momentous had occurred in my life and I suppose my conscious mind must have rationalised that event as falling in love with Alexandra.' His mouth curved in a grim smile. 'Only trouble was, I got the wrong woman. It was you I'd fallen in love with.'

Claire's nails bit painful grooves into the palms of her hands. Brett had loved her... He'd wanted to marry her. 'I had no idea,' she murmured, horrified by the trauma he was describing.

A muscle twitched convulsively in Brett's throat. 'How could you? You had as little idea of what I went through as I did of what had happened to you. But when those memories returned last night, they revived all the pain and anger of you leaving. That's all I could feel, that deep, drowning sense of loss. Realising on top of that that Emily was mine just about pushed me over the edge. Last night I had to get out of bed and leave you asleep for fear that I might actually harm you. I felt murderous.'

Claire shivered. 'No wonder you were so furious when you came back to Sandwood this morning.'

'This morning I wasn't thinking straight. I came back to Sandwood determined to make you suffer as I thought you'd made me suffer. That's not pleasant to say, but it's true. In my mind, I'd already built a dossier against you as thick as any encyclopaedia. I was determined to believe and think the worst.'

Claire skirted the sofa which separated them and tentatively placed a hand on his arm. 'I can understand that.'

'Can you?' Brett demanded rawly.

'Yes, you were hurt and upset and angry and you wanted to hit out at the person you thought was responsible. Me.'

'That doesn't make it right.'

'No,' Claire agreed. 'But it's only human. I felt the same when Alexandra first told me she'd seen my letters. I thought you must have shown them to her. I hated you for that. I felt totally betrayed. Besides, this morning you were right about some things. I should have told you the truth earlier... It was wrong of me not to.'

'You were frightened, I realise that now. Frightened of how I would react.'

Claire took a deep breath. 'At first I thought you might not even want to acknowledge Emily as yours, and later I was terrified you might try to take her away from me. I thought you didn't feel I was capable of looking after her properly.'

Brett's expression was bleak. 'My views on single parents have been coloured by my own experiences. I never told you about my own childhood so you couldn't have known what strong views it left me with. Our mother, Duncan's and mine, never wanted either of us.

She was a wealthy social butterfly, flitting from man to man, country to country. Children had no place in her world. She dumped both Duncan and me on our fathers when we were only a few years old. It left me very bitter about parents who neglect their responsibilities to their children. My father did his best, but I always felt there was something missing. I vowed I would never allow the same thing to happen to my children.'

'We won't,' Claire said softly, entwining her arms around his neck and holding him close.

Still Brett held himself rigid. 'Claire, what I said this morning about taking Emily from you if you didn't marry me... I should never have said that. I can't blackmail you into marriage. It wouldn't be fair.'

'I thought all was fair in love and war,' Claire murmured. 'And I do love you, very, very much.'

Brett shuddered, holding her away from him slightly. 'After everything that's happened, can you still love me? Can you still want to marry me?' he demanded fiercely.

'Just you try getting out of it,' Claire threatened softly. 'As soon as possible, you said, and that's what I'm holding you to. I can't wait to be Mrs Brett Jarrett.'

He crushed her to him then, his mouth swooping down to capture hers in a kiss that wrested almost every last gulp of air from her lungs. 'I love you so much,' he murmured huskily.

Suddenly a wail sounded from the other room, loud and protesting.

Claire eased herself away from Brett slightly and cocked an ear. 'You did say there were two of us in Emily's life now, darling...and since you do have several broken nights to make up for I think it's *your* turn to sort our daughter out.'

She grinned as she watched Brett making his way through to the smaller of the two bedrooms, and was still smiling when she entered the larger one.

Ten minutes later the wailing had stopped and Brett came in, pausing as he saw her curved enticingly, and obviously naked, beneath the sheets.

'I never knew you could sing Brahms's "Lullaby" so well,' she teased.

'You don't yet know half the things I can do very well indeed,' Brett drawled huskily.

'I can't wait to find out what they are,' she smiled provocatively.

'And I can't wait to show you,' Brett assured her, reaching the bed and drawing her into the strong, protective circle of his arms.

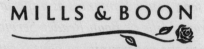

4 FREE

Romances and 2 FREE gifts just for you!

You can enjoy all the heartwarming emotion of true love for FREE! Discover the heartbreak and happiness, the emotion and the tenderness of the modern relationships in Mills & Boon Romances.

We'll send you 4 Romances as a special offer from Mills & Boon Reader Service, along with the opportunity to have 6 captivating new Romances delivered to your door each month.

Claim your FREE books and gifts overleaf...

An irresistible offer from Mills & Boon

Become a regular reader of Romances with Mills & Boon Reader Service and we'll welcome you with 4 books, a CUDDLY TEDDY and a special MYSTERY GIFT all absolutely FREE.

And then look forward to receiving 6 brand new Romances each month, delivered to your door hot off the presses, postage and packing FREE! Plus our free Newsletter featuring author news, competitions, special offers and much more.

This invitation comes with no strings attached. You may cancel or suspend your subscription at any time, and still keep your free books and gifts.

It's so easy. Send no money now. Simply fill in the coupon below and post it to -
Reader Service, FREEPOST, PO Box 236, Croydon, Surrey CR9 9EL.

NO STAMP REQUIRED

Free Books Coupon

Yes! Please rush me 4 FREE Romances and 2 FREE gifts! Please also reserve me a Reader Service subscription. If I decide to subscribe I can look forward to receiving 6 brand new Romances for just £10.80 each month, postage and packing FREE. If I decide not to subscribe I shall write to you within 10 days - I can keep the free books and gifts whatever I choose. I may cancel or suspend my subscription at any time. I am over 18 years of age.

Ms/Mrs/Miss/Mr _____   EP56R

Address _____

_____

Postcode _____ Signature _____

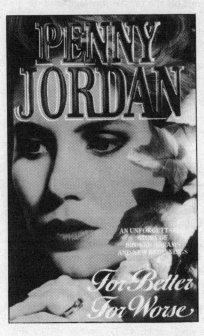

Next Month's Romances

Each month you can choose from a wide variety of romance with Mills & Boon. Below are the new titles to look out for next month, why not ask either Mills & Boon Reader Service or your Newsagent to reserve you a copy of the titles you want to buy – just tick the titles you would like and either post to Reader Service or take it to any Newsagent and ask them to order your books.

Please save me the following titles:	Please tick	√
DAWN SONG	Sara Craven	
FALLING IN LOVE	Charlotte Lamb	
MISTRESS OF DECEPTION	Miranda Lee	
POWERFUL STRANGER	Patricia Wilson	
SAVAGE DESTINY	Amanda Browning	
WEST OF BOHEMIA	Jessica Steele	
A HEARTLESS MARRIAGE	Helen Brooks	
ROSES IN THE NIGHT	Kay Gregory	
LADY BE MINE	Catherine Spencer	
SICILIAN SPRING	Sally Wentworth	
A SCANDALOUS AFFAIR	Stephanie Howard	
FLIGHT OF FANTASY	Valerie Parv	
RISK TO LOVE	Lynn Jacobs	
DARK DECEIVER	Alex Ryder	
SONG OF THE LORELEI	Lucy Gordon	
A TASTE OF HEAVEN	Carol Grace	

If you would like to order these books in addition to your regular subscription from Mills & Boon Reader Service please send £1.80 per title to: Mills & Boon Reader Service, Freepost, P.O. Box 236, Croydon, Surrey, CR9 9EL, quote your Subscriber No:.................................. (If applicable) and complete the name and address details below. Alternatively, these books are available from many local Newsagents including W.H.Smith, J.Menzies, Martins and other paperback stockists from 3 December 1993.

Name:...

Address:...

....Post Code:...........................

To Retailer: If you would like to stock M&B books please contact your regular book/magazine wholesaler for details.

You may be mailed with offers from other reputable companies as a result of this application.
If you would rather not take advantage of these opportunities please tick box ☐